# WELCOME to DEAD HOUSE

# Goosebumps®

# WELCOME to DEAD HOUSE

## R.L. STINE

**SCHOLASTIC INC.**

NEW YORK  TORONTO  LONDON  AUCKLAND
SYDNEY  MEXICO CITY  NEW DELHI  HONG KONG

ISBN: 978-0-545-15888-6

Goosebumps book series created by Parachute Press, Inc.
Copyright © 1992 by Scholastic Inc.

12  11  10  9  8  7  6  5  4  3          11  12  13  14  15/0

Printed in the U.S.A.
First printing, February 2010                                    40

"Behind the Screams" bonus material by Matthew D. Payne

Josh and I hated our new house.

Sure, it was big. It looked like a mansion compared to our old house. It was a tall redbrick house with a sloping black roof and rows of windows framed by black shutters.

*It's so dark*, I thought, studying it from the street. The whole house was covered in darkness, as if it were hiding in the shadows of the gnarled old trees that bent over it.

It was the middle of July, but dead brown leaves blanketed the front yard. Our sneakers crunched over them as we trudged up the gravel driveway.

Tall weeds poked up everywhere through the dead leaves. Thick clumps of weeds had completely overgrown an old flower bed beside the front porch.

*This house is creepy*, I thought unhappily.

Josh must have been thinking the same thing.

Looking up at the old house, we both groaned loudly.

Mr. Dawes, the friendly young man from the local real estate office, stopped near the front walk and turned around.

"Everything okay?" he asked, staring first at Josh, then at me, with his crinkly blue eyes.

"Josh and Amanda aren't happy about moving," Dad explained, tucking his shirttail in. Dad is a little overweight, and his shirts always seem to be coming untucked.

"It's hard for kids," my mother added, smiling at Mr. Dawes, her hands shoved into her jeans pockets as she continued up to the front door. "You know. Leaving all of their friends behind. Moving to a strange new place."

"Strange is right," Josh said, shaking his head. "This house is gross."

Mr. Dawes chuckled. "It's an old house, that's for sure," he said, patting Josh on the shoulder.

"It just needs some work, Josh," Dad said, smiling at Mr. Dawes. "No one has lived in it for a while, so it'll take some fixing up."

"Look how big it is," Mom added, smoothing back her straight black hair and smiling at Josh. "We'll have room for a den and maybe a rec room, too. You'd like that — wouldn't you, Amanda?"

2

I shrugged. A cold breeze made me shiver. It was actually a beautiful, hot summer day. But the closer we got to the house, the colder I felt.

I guessed it was because of all the tall old trees.

I was wearing white tennis shorts and a sleeveless blue T-shirt. It had been hot in the car. But now I was freezing. *Maybe it'll be warmer in the house*, I thought.

"How old are they?" Mr. Dawes asked Mom, stepping onto the front porch.

"Amanda is twelve," Mom answered. "And Josh turned eleven last month."

"They look so much alike," Mr. Dawes told Mom.

I couldn't decide if that was a compliment or not. I guess it's true. Josh and I are both tall and thin and have curly brown hair like Dad's and dark brown eyes. Everyone says we have "serious" faces.

"I really want to go home," Josh said, his voice cracking. "I hate this place."

My brother is the most impatient kid in the world. And when he makes up his mind about something, that's it. He's a little spoiled. At least, I think so. Whenever he makes a big fuss about something, he usually gets his way.

We may look alike, but we're really not that similar. I'm a lot more patient than Josh is. A lot more sensible. Probably because I'm older and because I'm a girl.

Josh had grabbed Dad's hand and was trying to pull him back to the car. "Let's go. Come on, Dad. Let's go."

I knew this was one time Josh wouldn't get his way. We were moving to this house. No doubt about it. After all, the house was absolutely free. A great-uncle of Dad's, a man we didn't even know, had died and left the house to Dad in his will.

I'll never forget the look on Dad's face when he got the letter from the lawyer. He let out a loud whoop and began dancing around the living room. Josh and I thought he'd flipped or something.

"My great-uncle Charles has left us a house in his will," Dad explained, reading and rereading the letter. "It's in a town called Dark Falls."

"Huh?" Josh and I cried. "Where's Dark Falls?"

Dad shrugged.

"I don't remember your uncle Charles," Mom said, moving behind Dad to read the letter over his shoulder.

"Neither do I," admitted Dad. "But he must've been a great guy! Wow! This sounds like an incredible house!" He grabbed Mom's hands and began dancing happily with her across the living room.

Dad sure was excited. He'd been looking for an excuse to quit his boring office job and devote all of his time to his writing career. This house — absolutely free — would be just the excuse he needed.

And now, a week later, here we were in Dark Falls, a four-hour drive from our home, seeing our new house for the first time. We hadn't even gone inside, and Josh was trying to drag Dad back to the car.

"Josh — stop pulling me," Dad snapped impatiently, struggling to tug his hand out of Josh's grasp.

Dad glanced helplessly at Mr. Dawes. I could see that he was embarrassed by how Josh was carrying on. I decided maybe I could help.

"Let go, Josh," I said quietly, grabbing him by the shoulder. "We promised we'd give Dark Falls a chance — remember?"

"I already gave it a chance," Josh whined, not letting go of Dad's hand. "This house is old and ugly and I hate it."

"You haven't even gone inside," Dad said angrily.

"Yes. Let's go in," Mr. Dawes urged, staring at Josh.

"I'm staying outside," Josh insisted.

He can be really stubborn sometimes. I felt just as unhappy as Josh looking at this dark old house. But I'd never carry on the way Josh was.

"Josh, don't you want to pick out your own room?" Mom asked.

"No," Josh muttered.

He and I both glanced up to the second floor. There were two large bay windows side by side up there. They looked like two dark eyes staring back at us.

"How long have you lived in your present house?" Mr. Dawes asked Dad.

Dad had to think for a second. "About fourteen years," he answered. "The kids have lived there for their whole lives."

"Moving is always hard," Mr. Dawes said sympathetically, turning his gaze on me. "You know, Amanda, I moved here to Dark Falls just a few months ago. I didn't like it much, either, at first. But now I wouldn't live anywhere else." He winked at me. He had a cute dimple in his chin when he smiled. "Let's go inside. It's really quite nice. You'll be surprised."

All of us followed Mr. Dawes, except Josh. "Are there other kids on this block?" Josh demanded. He made it sound more like a challenge than a question.

Mr. Dawes nodded. "The school's just two blocks away," he said, pointing up the street.

"See?" Mom quickly cut in. "A short walk to school. No more long bus rides every morning."

"I *liked* the bus," Josh insisted.

His mind was made up. He wasn't going to give my parents a break, even though we'd both promised to be open-minded about this move.

6

I don't know what Josh thought he had to gain by being such a pain. I mean, Dad already had plenty to worry about. For one thing, he hadn't been able to sell our old house yet.

I didn't like the idea of moving. But I knew that inheriting this big house was a great opportunity for us. We were so cramped in our little house. And once Dad managed to sell the old place, we wouldn't have to worry at all about money anymore.

Josh should at least give it a chance. That's what I thought.

Suddenly, from our car at the foot of the driveway, we heard Petey barking and howling and making a fuss.

Petey is our dog, a white curly-haired terrier, cute as a button, and usually well-behaved. He never minded being left in the car. But now he was yowling and yapping at full volume and scratching at the car window, desperate to get out.

"Petey — quiet! Quiet!" I shouted. Petey usually listened to me.

But not this time.

"I'm going to let him out!" Josh declared, and took off down the driveway toward the car.

"No. Wait —" Dad called.

But I don't think Josh could hear him over Petey's wails.

"Might as well let the dog explore," Mr. Dawes said. "It's going to be his house, too."

A few seconds later, Petey came charging across the lawn, kicking up brown leaves, yipping excitedly as he ran up to us. He jumped on all of us as if he hadn't seen us in weeks and then, to our surprise, he started growling menacingly and barking at Mr. Dawes.

"Petey — stop!" Mom yelled.

"He's never done this," Dad said apologetically. "Really. He's usually very friendly."

"He probably smells something on me. Another dog, maybe," Mr. Dawes said, loosening his striped tie, looking warily at our growling dog.

Finally, Josh grabbed Petey around the middle and lifted him away from Mr. Dawes. "Stop it, Petey," Josh scolded, holding the dog up close to his face so that they were nose to nose. "Mr. Dawes is our friend."

Petey whimpered and licked Josh's face. After a short while, Josh set him back down on the ground. Petey looked up at Mr. Dawes, then at me, then decided to go sniffing around the yard, letting his nose lead the way.

"Let's go inside," Mr. Dawes urged, moving a hand through his short blond hair. He unlocked the front door and pushed it open.

Mr. Dawes held the screen door open for us. I started to follow my parents into the house.

"I'll stay out here with Petey," Josh insisted from the walk.

Dad started to protest but changed his mind. "Okay. Fine," he said, sighing and shaking his head. "I'm not going to argue with you. Don't come in. You can *live* outside if you want." He sounded really exasperated.

"I want to stay with Petey," Josh said again, watching Petey nose his way through the overgrown flower bed.

Mr. Dawes followed us into the hallway, gently closing the screen door behind him, giving Josh a final glance. "He'll be fine," he said softly, smiling at Mom.

"He can be so stubborn sometimes," Mom said apologetically. She peeked into the living room. "I'm really sorry about Petey. I don't know what got into that dog."

"No problem. Let's start in the living room," Mr. Dawes said, leading the way. "I think you'll be pleasantly surprised by how spacious it is. Of course, it needs work."

He took us on a tour of every room in the house. I was beginning to get excited. The house was really kind of neat. There were so many rooms and so many closets. And my room was huge and had its own bathroom and an old-fashioned window seat where I could sit and look down at the street.

I wished Josh had come inside with us. If he could see how great the house was inside, I knew he'd start to cheer up.

ouldn't believe how many rooms there were. re was even a finished attic filled with old fur- ture and stacks of old, mysterious cartons we could explore.

We must have been inside for at least half an hour. I didn't really keep track of the time. I think all three of us were feeling cheered up.

"Well, I think I've shown you everything," Mr. Dawes said, glancing at his watch. He led the way to the front door.

"Wait — I want to take one more look at my room," I told them excitedly. I started up the stairs, taking them two at a time. "I'll be down in a second."

"Hurry, dear. I'm sure Mr. Dawes has other appointments," Mom called after me.

I reached the second-floor landing and hurried down the narrow hallway and into my new room. "Wow!" I said aloud, and the word echoed faintly against the empty walls.

It was so big. And I loved the bay window with the window seat. I walked over to it and peered out. Through the trees, I could see our car in the driveway and, beyond it, a house that looked a lot like ours across the street.

*I'm going to put my bed against that wall across from the window,* I thought happily. *And my desk can go over there. I'll have room for a computer now!*

I took one more look at my long walk-in closet, which had a light in the ceiling and wide shelves against the back wall.

I was heading to the door, thinking about which of my posters I wanted to bring with me, when I saw the boy.

He stood in the doorway for just a second. And then he turned and disappeared down the hall.

"Josh?" I cried. "Hey — come look!"

With a shock, I realized it wasn't Josh.

For one thing, the boy had blond hair.

"Hey!" I called and ran to the hallway, stopping just outside my bedroom door, looking both ways. "Who's there?"

But the long hall was empty. All of the doors were closed.

"Whoa, Amanda," I said aloud.

Was I seeing things?

Mom and Dad were calling from downstairs. I took one last look down the dark corridor, then hurried to rejoin them.

"Hey, Mr. Dawes," I called as I ran down the stairs, "is this house haunted?"

He chuckled. The question seemed to strike him funny. "No. Sorry," he said, looking at me with those crinkly blue eyes. "No ghost included. A lot of old houses around here are said to be haunted. But I'm afraid this isn't one of them."

"I — I thought I saw something," I said, feeling a little foolish.

"Probably just shadows," Mom said. "With all the trees, this house is so dark."

"Why don't you run outside and tell Josh about the house," Dad suggested, tucking in the front of his shirt. "Your mom and I have some things to talk over with Mr. Dawes."

"Yes, master," I said with a little bow, and obediently ran out to tell Josh all about what he had missed. "Hey, Josh," I called, eagerly searching the yard. "Josh?"

My heart sank.

Josh and Petey were gone.

"Josh! Josh!"

First I called Josh. Then I called Petey. But there was no sign of either of them.

I ran down to the bottom of the driveway and peered into the car, but they weren't there. Mom and Dad were still inside talking with Mr. Dawes. I looked along the street in both directions, but there was no sign of them.

"Josh! Hey, Josh!"

Finally, Mom and Dad came hurrying out the front door, looking alarmed. I guess they heard my shouts. "I can't find Josh or Petey!" I yelled up to them from the street.

"Maybe they're around back," Dad shouted down to me.

I headed up the driveway, kicking away dead leaves as I ran. It was sunny down on the street, but as soon as I entered our yard, I was back in the shade, and it was immediately cool again.

"Hey, Josh! Josh — where are you?"

Why did I feel so scared? It was perfectly natural for Josh to wander off. He did it all the time.

I ran full speed along the side of the house. Tall trees leaned over the house on this side, blocking out nearly all of the sunlight.

The backyard was bigger than I'd expected, a long rectangle that sloped gradually down to a wooden fence at the back. Just like the front, this yard was a mass of tall weeds, poking up through a thick covering of brown leaves. A stone birdbath had toppled onto its side. Beyond it, I could see the side of the garage, a dark brick building that matched the house.

"Hey — Josh!"

He wasn't back here. I stopped and searched the ground for footprints or a sign that he had run through the thick leaves.

"Well?" Out of breath, Dad came jogging up to me.

"No sign of him," I said, surprised at how worried I felt.

"Did you check the car?" He sounded more angry than worried.

"Yes. It's the first place I looked." I gave the backyard a last quick search. "I don't believe Josh would just take off."

"I do," Dad said, rolling his eyes. "You know your brother when he doesn't get his way. Maybe he wants us to think he's run away from home." He frowned.

14

"Where is he?" Mom asked as we returned to the front of the house.

Dad and I both shrugged. "Maybe he made a friend and wandered off," Dad said. He raised a hand and scratched his curly brown hair. I could tell that he was starting to worry, too.

"We've *got* to find him," Mom said, gazing down to the street. "He doesn't know this neighborhood at all. He probably wandered off and got lost."

Mr. Dawes locked the front door and stepped down off the porch, pocketing the keys. "He couldn't have gotten far," he said, giving Mom a reassuring smile. "Let's drive around the block. I'm sure we'll find him."

Mom shook her head and glanced nervously at Dad. "I'll kill him," she muttered. Dad patted her on the shoulder.

Mr. Dawes opened the trunk of the small Honda, pulled off his dark blazer, and tossed it inside. Then he took out a wide-brimmed black cowboy hat and put it on his head.

"Hey — that's quite a hat," Dad said, climbing into the front passenger seat.

"Keeps the sun away," Mr. Dawes said, sliding behind the wheel and slamming the car door.

Mom and I got in back. Glancing over at her, I saw that Mom was as worried as I was.

We headed down the block in silence, all four of us staring out the car windows. The houses we passed all seemed old. Most of them were even bigger than our house. All of them seemed to be in better condition, nicely painted with neat, well-trimmed lawns.

I didn't see any people in the houses or yards, and there was no one on the street.

*It certainly is a* quiet *neighborhood*, I thought. *And shady.* The houses all seemed to be surrounded by tall leafy trees. The front yards we drove slowly past all seemed to be bathed in shade. The street was the only sunny place, a narrow gold ribbon that ran through the shadows on both sides.

*Maybe that's why it's called Dark Falls,* I thought.

"Where is that son of mine?" Dad asked, staring hard out the windshield.

"I'll kill him. I really will," Mom muttered. It wasn't the first time she had said that about Josh.

We had gone around the block twice. No sign of him.

Mr. Dawes suggested we drive around the next few blocks, and Dad quickly agreed. "Hope I don't get lost. I'm new here, too," Mr. Dawes said, turning a corner. "Hey, there's the school," he announced, pointing out the window at a tall red-brick building. It looked very old-fashioned, with white columns on both sides of the double front doors. "Of course, it's closed now," Mr. Dawes added.

My eyes searched the fenced-in playground behind the school. It was empty. No one there.

"Could Josh have walked here?" Mom asked, her voice tight and higher than usual.

"Josh doesn't walk," Dad said, rolling his eyes. "He runs."

"We'll find him," Mr. Dawes said confidently, tapping his fingers on the wheel as he steered.

We turned a corner onto another shady block. A street sign read CEMETERY DRIVE, and sure enough, a large cemetery rose up in front of us. Granite gravestones rolled along a low hill that sloped down and then up again onto a large flat stretch, also marked with rows of low grave markers and monuments.

A few shrubs dotted the cemetery, but there weren't many trees. As we drove slowly past, the gravestones passing by in a blur on the left, I realized that this was the sunniest spot I had seen in the whole town.

"There's your son." Mr. Dawes, pointing out the window, stopped the car suddenly.

"Oh, thank goodness!" Mom exclaimed, leaning down to see out the window on my side of the car.

Sure enough, there was Josh, running wildly along a crooked row of low white gravestones. "What's he doing *here*?" I asked, pushing open my car door.

I got out of the car, took a few steps onto the grass, and called to him. At first, he didn't react

17

to my shouts. He seemed to be ducking and dodging through the tombstones. He would run in one direction, then cut to the side, then head in another direction.

Why was he doing that?

I took another few steps — and then stopped, gripped with fear.

I suddenly realized why Josh was darting and ducking like that, running so wildly through the tombstones. He was being chased.

Someone — or something — was after him.

Then, as I took a few reluctant steps toward Josh, watching him bend low, then change directions, his arms outstretched as he ran, I realized I had it completely backward.

Josh wasn't being chased. Josh was *chasing*.

He was chasing Petey.

Okay, okay. So sometimes my imagination runs away with me. Running through an old graveyard like this — even in bright daylight — it's only natural that a person might start to have weird thoughts.

I called to Josh again, and this time he heard me and turned around. He looked worried. "Amanda — come help me!" he cried.

"Josh, what's the matter?" I ran as fast as I could to catch up with him, but he kept darting through the gravestones, moving from row to row.

"Help!"

"Josh — what's wrong?" I turned and saw that Mom and Dad were right behind me.

"It's Petey," Josh explained, out of breath. "I can't get him to stop. I caught him once, but he pulled away from me."

"Petey! Petey!" Dad started calling the dog. But Petey was moving from stone to stone, sniffing each one, then running to the next.

"How did you get all the way over here?" Dad asked as he caught up with my brother.

"I had to follow Petey," Josh explained, still looking very worried. "He just took off. One second he was sniffing around that flower bed in our front yard. The next second, he just started to run. He wouldn't stop when I called. Wouldn't even look back. He kept running till he got here. I had to follow. I was afraid he'd get lost."

Josh stopped and gratefully let Dad take over the chase. "I don't know what that dumb dog's problem is," he said to me. "He's just *weird*."

It took Dad a few tries, but he finally managed to grab Petey and pick him up off the ground. Our little terrier gave a halfhearted yelp of protest, then allowed himself to be carried away.

We all trooped back to the car on the side of the road. Mr. Dawes was waiting there. "Maybe you'd better get a leash for that dog," he said, looking very concerned.

"Petey's never been on a leash," Josh protested, wearily climbing into the backseat.

"Well, we might have to try one for a while," Dad said quietly. "Especially if he keeps running away." Dad tossed Petey into the backseat. The dog eagerly curled up in Josh's arms.

The rest of us piled into the car, and Mr. Dawes drove us back to his office, a tiny, white, flat-roofed building at the end of a row of small offices. As we rode, I reached over and stroked the back of Petey's head.

*Why did the dog run away like that?* I wondered. Petey had never done that before.

I guessed that Petey was also upset about our moving. After all, Petey had spent his whole life in our old house. He probably felt a lot like Josh and I did about having to pack up and move and never see the old neighborhood again.

The new house, the new streets, and all the new smells must have freaked out the poor dog. Josh wanted to run away from the whole idea. And so did Petey.

Anyway, that was my theory.

Mr. Dawes parked the car in front of his tiny office, shook Dad's hand, and gave him a business card. "You can come by next week," he told Mom and Dad. "I'll have all the legal work done by then. After you sign the papers, you can move in anytime."

He pushed open the car door and, giving us all a final smile, prepared to climb out.

"Compton Dawes," Mom said, reading the white business card over Dad's shoulder. "That's an unusual name. Is Compton an old family name?"

Mr. Dawes shook his head. "No," he said, "I'm the only Compton in my family. I have no idea where the name comes from. No idea at all. Maybe my parents didn't know how to spell Charlie!"

Chuckling at his terrible joke, he climbed out of the car, lowered the wide black Stetson hat on his head, pulled his blazer from the trunk, and disappeared into the small white building.

Dad climbed behind the wheel, moving the seat back to make room for his big stomach. Mom got up front, and we started the long drive home. "I guess you and Petey had quite an adventure today," Mom said to Josh, rolling up her window because Dad had turned on the air conditioner.

"I guess," Josh said without enthusiasm. Petey was sound asleep in his lap, snoring quietly.

"You're going to love your room," I told Josh. "The whole house is great. Really."

Josh stared at me thoughtfully but didn't answer.

I poked him in the ribs with my elbow. "Say something. Did you hear what I said?"

But the weird, thoughtful look didn't fade from Josh's face.

The next couple of weeks crawled by. I walked around the house thinking about how I'd never see my room again, how I'd never eat breakfast in this kitchen again, how I'd never watch TV in the living room again. Morbid stuff like that.

I had this sick feeling when the movers came one afternoon and delivered a tall stack of cartons. Time to pack up. It was really happening. Even though it was the middle of the day, I went up to my room and flopped down on my bed. I didn't nap or anything. I just stared at the ceiling for more than an hour, and all these wild, unconnected thoughts ran through my head, like a dream, only I was awake.

I wasn't the only one who was nervous about the move. Mom and Dad were snapping at each other over nothing at all. One morning they had a big fight over whether the bacon was too crispy or not.

In a way, it was funny to see them being so childish. Josh was acting really sullen all the time. He hardly spoke a word to anyone. And Petey sulked, too. That dumb dog wouldn't even pick himself up and come over to me when I had some table scraps for him.

I guess the hardest part about moving was saying good-bye to my friends. Carol and Amy were away at camp, so I had to write to them. But Kathy was home, and she was my oldest and best friend, and the hardest to say good-bye to.

I think some people were surprised that Kathy and I had stayed such good friends. For one thing, we look so different. I'm tall and thin and dark, and she's fair-skinned, with long blond hair, and a little chubby. But we've been friends since preschool, and best best friends since fourth grade.

When she came over the night before the move, we were both terribly awkward. "Kathy, you shouldn't be nervous," I told her. "You're not the one who's moving away forever."

"It's not like you're moving to China or something," she answered, chewing hard on her bubble gum. "Dark Falls is only four hours away, Amanda. We'll see each other a lot."

"Yeah, I guess," I said. But I didn't believe it. Four hours away was as bad as being in China, as far as I was concerned. "I guess we can still talk on the phone," I said glumly.

She blew a small green bubble, then sucked it back into her mouth. "Yeah. Sure," she said, pretending to be enthusiastic. "You're lucky, you know. Moving out of this crummy neighborhood to a big house."

"It's *not* a crummy neighborhood," I insisted. I don't know why I was defending the neighborhood. I never had before. One of our favorite pastimes was thinking of places we'd rather be growing up.

"School won't be the same without you," she sighed, curling her legs under her on the chair. "Who's going to slip me the answers in math?"

I laughed. "I always slipped you the *wrong* answers."

"But it was the thought that counted," Kathy said. And then she groaned. "Ugh. Junior high. Is your new junior high part of the high school or part of the elementary school?"

I made a disgusted face. "Everything's in one building. It's a small town, remember? There's no separate high school. At least, I didn't see one."

"Bummer," she said.

Bummer was right.

We chatted for hours. Until Kathy's mom called and said it was time for her to come home.

Then we hugged. I had made up my mind that I wouldn't cry, but I could feel the big, hot tears forming in the corners of my eyes. And then they were running down my cheeks.

"I'm so miserable!" I wailed.

I had planned to be really controlled and mature. But Kathy was my best friend, after all, and what could I do?

We made a promise that we'd always be together on our birthdays — no matter what. We'd force our parents to make sure we didn't miss each other's birthdays.

And then we hugged again. And Kathy said, "Don't worry. We'll see each other a lot. Really." And she had tears in her eyes, too.

She turned and ran out the door. The screen door slammed hard behind her. I stood there staring out into the darkness until Petey came

scampering in, his toenails clicking across the lino-
leum, and started to lick my hand.

The next morning, moving day, was a rainy
Saturday. Not a downpour. No thunder or lightning. But just enough rain and wind to make the
long drive slow and unpleasant.

The sky seemed to get darker as we neared the
new neighborhood. The heavy trees bent low over
the street. "Slow down, Jack," Mom warned
shrilly. "The street is really slick."

But Dad was in a hurry to get to the house
before the moving van did. "They'll just put the
stuff anywhere if we're not there to supervise,"
he explained.

Josh, beside me in the backseat, was being a
real pain, as usual. He kept complaining that
he was thirsty. When that didn't get results, he
started whining that he was starving. But we had
all had a big breakfast — so that didn't get any
reaction, either.

He just wanted attention, of course. I kept trying to cheer him up by telling him how great the
house was inside and how big his room was. He
still hadn't seen it.

But he didn't want to be cheered up. He started
wrestling with Petey, getting the poor dog all
worked up, until Dad had to shout at him to stop.

"Let's all try really hard not to get on each
other's nerves," Mom suggested.

Dad laughed. "Good idea, dear."

"Don't make fun of me," she snapped.

They started to argue about who was more exhausted from all the packing. Petey stood up on his hind legs and started to howl at the back window.

"Can't you shut him up?" Mom screamed.

I pulled Petey down, but he struggled back up and started howling again. "He's never done this before," I said.

"Just get him quiet!" Mom insisted.

I pulled Petey down by his hind legs, and Josh started to howl. Mom turned around and gave him a dirty look. Josh didn't stop howling, though. He thought he was a riot.

Finally, Dad pulled the car up the driveway of the new house. The tires crunched over the wet gravel. Rain pounded on the roof.

"Home sweet home," Mom said. I couldn't tell if she was being sarcastic or not. I think she was really glad the long car ride was over.

"At least we beat the movers," Dad said, glancing at his watch. Then his expression changed. "Hope they're not lost."

"It's as dark as night out there," Josh complained.

Petey was jumping up and down in my lap, desperate to get out of the car. He was usually a good traveler. But once the car stopped, he wanted out immediately.

27

I opened my car door and he leaped onto the driveway with a splash and started to run in a wild zigzag across the front yard.

"At least *someone's* glad to be here," Josh said quietly.

Dad ran up to the porch and, fumbling with the unfamiliar keys, managed to get the front door open. Then he motioned for us to come into the house.

Mom and Josh ran across the walk, eager to get in out of the rain. I closed the car door behind me and started to jog after them.

But something caught my eye. I stopped and looked up to the twin bay windows above the porch.

I held a hand over my eyebrows to shield my eyes and squinted through the rain.

Yes. I saw it.

A face. In the window on the left.

The boy.

The same boy was up there, staring down at me.

"Wipe your feet! Don't track mud on the nice clean floors!" Mom called. Her voice echoed against the bare walls of the empty living room.

I stepped into the hallway. The house smelled of paint. The painters had just finished on Thursday. It was hot in the house, much hotter than outside.

"This kitchen light won't go on," Dad called from the back. "Did the painters turn off the electricity or something?"

"How should I know?" Mom shouted back.

Their voices sounded so loud in the big, empty house.

"Mom — there's someone upstairs!" I cried, wiping my feet on the new welcome mat and hurrying into the living room.

She was at the window, staring out at the rain, looking for the movers probably. She spun around as I came in. "What?"

"There's a boy upstairs. I saw him in the window," I said, struggling to catch my breath.

Josh entered the room from the back hallway. He'd probably been with Dad. He laughed. "Is someone already living here?"

"There's no one upstairs," Mom said, rolling her eyes. "Are you two going to give me a break today, or what?"

"What did *I* do?" Josh whined.

"Listen, Amanda, we're all a little on edge today —" Mom started.

But I interrupted her. "I saw his face, Mom. In the window. I'm not crazy, you know."

"Says who?" Josh cracked.

"Amanda!" Mom bit her lower lip, the way she always did when she was exasperated. "You saw a reflection of something. Of a tree probably." She turned back to the window. The rain was coming down in sheets now, the wind driving it noisily against the large picture window.

I ran to the stairway, cupped my hands over my mouth, and shouted up to the second floor, "Who's up there?"

No answer.

"Who's up there?" I called, a little louder.

Mom had her hands over her ears. "Amanda — please!"

Josh had disappeared into the dining room. He was finally exploring the house.

"There's someone up there," I insisted and, impulsively, I started up the wooden stairway, my sneakers thudding loudly on the bare steps.

"Amanda —" I heard Mom call after me.

But I was too angry to stop. Why didn't she believe me? Why did she have to say it was a reflection of a tree I saw up there?

I was curious. I had to know who was upstairs. I had to prove Mom wrong. I had to show her I hadn't seen a stupid reflection. I guess I can be pretty stubborn, too. Maybe it's a family trait.

The stairs squeaked and creaked under me as I climbed. I didn't feel at all scared until I reached the second-floor landing. Then I suddenly had this heavy feeling in the pit of my stomach.

I stopped, breathing hard, leaning on the banister.

Who could it be? A burglar? A bored neighborhood kid who had broken into an empty house for a thrill?

*Maybe I shouldn't be up here alone,* I realized.
*Maybe the boy in the window was dangerous.*

"Anybody up here?" I called, my voice suddenly trembly and weak.

Still leaning against the banister, I listened.

And I could hear footsteps scampering across the hallway.

No.

Not footsteps.

The rain. That's what it was. The patter of rain against the slate-shingled roof.

For some reason, the sound made me feel a little calmer. I let go of the banister and stepped into the long, narrow hallway. It was dark up here, except for a rectangle of gray light from a small window at the other end.

I took a few steps, the old wooden floorboards creaking noisily beneath me. "Anybody up here?"

Again no answer.

I stepped up to the first doorway on my left. The door was closed. The smell of fresh paint was suffocating. There was a light switch on the wall near the door. *Maybe it's for the hall light*, I thought. I clicked it on. But nothing happened.

"Anybody here?"

My hand was trembling as I grabbed the door-knob. It felt warm in my hand. And damp.

I turned it and, taking a deep breath, pushed open the door.

I peered into the room. Gray light filtered in through the bay window. A flash of lightning made me jump back. The thunder that followed was a dull, distant roar.

Slowly, carefully, I took a step into the room. Then another.

No sign of anyone.

This was a guest bedroom. Or it could be Josh's room if he decided he liked it.

Another flash of lightning. The sky seemed to be darkening. It was pitch-black out there even though it was just after lunchtime.

I backed into the hall. The next room down was going to be mine. It also had a bay window that looked down on the front yard.

Was the boy I saw staring down at me in *my* room?

I crept down the hall, letting my hand run along the wall for some reason, and stopped outside my door, which was also closed.

Taking a deep breath, I knocked on the door. "Who's in there?" I called.

I listened.

Silence.

Then a clap of thunder, closer than the last. I froze as if I were paralyzed, holding my breath. It was so hot up here, hot and damp. And the smell of paint was making me dizzy.

I grabbed the doorknob. "Anybody in there?"

I started to turn the knob — when the boy crept up from behind and grabbed my shoulder.

I couldn't breathe. I couldn't cry out.

My heart seemed to stop. My chest felt as if it were about to explode.

With a desperate, terrified effort, I spun around.

"Josh!" I shrieked. "You scared me to death! I thought —"

He let go of me and took a step back. "Gotcha!" he declared, and then started to laugh, a high-pitched laugh that echoed down the long, bare hallway.

My heart was pounding hard now. My forehead throbbed. "You're not funny," I said angrily. I shoved him against the wall. "You really scared me."

He laughed and rolled around on the floor. He's really a sicko. I tried to shove him again but missed.

Angrily, I turned away from him — just in time to see my bedroom door slowly swinging open.

I gasped in disbelief. And froze, gaping at the moving door.

Josh stopped laughing and stood up, immediately serious, his dark eyes wide with fright.

I could hear someone moving inside the room.

I could hear whispering.

Excited giggles.

"Who — who's there?" I managed to stammer in a high little voice I didn't recognize.

The door, creaking loudly, opened a bit more, then started to close.

"Who's there?" I demanded, a bit more forcefully.

Again, I could hear whispering, someone moving about.

Josh had backed up against the wall and was edging away toward the stairs. He had an expression on his face I'd never seen before — sheer terror.

The door, creaking like a door in a movie haunted house, closed a little more.

Josh was nearly to the stairway. He was staring at me, violently motioning with his hand for me to follow.

But instead, I stepped forward, grabbed the doorknob, and pushed the door open hard.

It didn't resist.

I let go of the doorknob and stood blocking the doorway. "Who's there?"

The room was empty.

Thunder crashed.

It took me a few seconds to realize what was making the door move. The window on the opposite wall had been left open several inches. The gusting wind through the open window must have been opening and closing the door. I guessed that also explained the other sounds I heard inside the room, the sounds I thought were whispers.

Who had left the window open? The painters, probably.

I took a deep breath and let it out slowly, waiting for my pounding heart to settle down to normal.

Feeling a little foolish, I walked quickly to the window and pushed it shut.

"Amanda — are you all right?" Josh whispered from the hallway.

I started to answer him. But then I had a better idea.

He had practically scared me to death a few minutes before. Why not give *him* a little scare? He deserved it.

So I didn't answer him.

I could hear him take a few timid steps closer to my room. "Amanda? Amanda? You okay?"

I tiptoed over to my closet, pulled the door open a third of the way. Then I lay down flat on the floor, on my back, with my head and shoulders hidden inside the closet and the rest of me out in the room.

"Amanda?" Josh sounded very scared.

"Ohhhhh," I moaned loudly.

I knew when he saw me sprawled on the floor like this, he'd totally freak out!

"Amanda — what's happening?"

He was in the doorway now. He'd see me any second now, lying in the dark room, my head hidden from view, the lightning flashing impressively and the thunder cracking outside the old window.

I took a deep breath and held it to keep from giggling.

"Amanda?" he whispered. And then he must have seen me, because he uttered a loud "Huh?!" And I heard him gasp.

And then he screamed at the top of his lungs. I heard him running down the hall to the stairway, shrieking, "Mom! Dad!" And I heard his sneakers thudding down the wooden stairs, with him screaming and calling all the way down.

I snickered to myself. Then, before I could pull myself up, I felt a rough, warm tongue licking my face.

"Petey!"

He was licking my cheeks, licking my eyelids, licking me frantically, as if he were trying to revive me, or as if to let me know that everything was okay.

"Oh, Petey! Petey!" I cried, laughing and throwing my arms around the sweet dog. "Stop! You're getting me all sticky!"

But he wouldn't stop. He kept on licking fiercely.

*The poor dog is nervous, too,* I thought.

"Come on, Petey, shape up," I told him, holding his panting face away with both my hands. "There's nothing to be nervous about. This new place is going to be fun. You'll see."

That night, I was smiling to myself as I fluffed up my pillow and slid into bed. I was thinking about how terrified Josh had been that afternoon, how frightened he looked even after I came prancing down the stairs, perfectly okay. How angry he was that I'd fooled him.

Of course, Mom and Dad didn't think it was funny. They were both nervous and upset because the moving van had just arrived, an hour late. They forced Josh and me to call a truce. No more scaring each other.

"It's hard *not* to get scared in this creepy old place," Josh muttered. But we reluctantly agreed not to play any more jokes on each other, if we could possibly help it.

The men, complaining about the rain, started carrying in all of our furniture. Josh and I helped show them where we wanted stuff in our rooms. They dropped my dresser on the stairs, but it only got a small scratch.

The furniture looked strange and small in this big house. Josh and I tried to stay out of the way while Mom and Dad worked all day, arranging things, emptying cartons, putting clothes away. Mom even managed to get the curtains hung in my room.

What a day!

Now, a little after ten o'clock, trying to get to sleep for the first time in my new room, I turned onto my side, then onto my back. Even though this was my old bed, I couldn't get comfortable.

Everything seemed so different, so wrong. The bed didn't face the same direction as in my old bedroom. The walls were bare. I hadn't had time to hang any of my posters. The room seemed so large and empty. The shadows seemed so much darker.

My back started to itch, and then I suddenly felt itchy all over. *The bed is filled with bugs!* I thought, sitting up. But of course that was ridiculous. It was my same old bed with clean sheets.

I forced myself to settle back down and closed my eyes. Sometimes when I can't get to sleep, I count silently by twos, picturing each number in my mind as I think it. It usually helps to clear my mind so that I can drift off to sleep.

I tried it now, burying my face in the pillow, picturing the numbers rolling past . . . 4 . . . 6 . . . 8 . . .

I yawned loudly, still wide-awake at two-twenty.

*I'm going to be awake forever*, I thought. *I'm never going to be able to sleep in this new room.*

But then I must have drifted off without realizing it. I don't know how long I slept. An hour or two at the most. It was a light, uncomfortable sleep. Then something woke me. I sat straight up, startled.

Despite the heat of the room, I felt cold all over. Looking down to the end of the bed, I saw that I had kicked off the sheet and light blanket. With a groan, I reached down for them but then froze.

I heard whispers.

Someone was whispering across the room.

"Who — who's there?" My voice was a whisper, too, tiny and frightened.

I grabbed my covers and pulled them up to my chin.

I heard more whispers. The room came into focus as my eyes adjusted to the dim light.

The curtains. The long, sheer curtains from my old room that my mother had hung that afternoon were fluttering at the window.

So. That explained the whispers. The billowing curtains must have woken me up.

A soft gray light floated in from outside. The curtains cast moving shadows onto the foot of my bed.

Yawning, I stretched and climbed out of bed. I felt chilled all over as I crept across the wooden floor to close the window.

As I came near, the curtains stopped billowing and floated back into place. I pushed them aside and reached out to close the window.

"Oh!"

I uttered a soft cry when I realized that the window *was* closed.

But how could the curtains flutter like that with the window closed? I stood there for a while, staring out at the grays of the night. There wasn't much of a draft. The window seemed pretty airtight.

Had I imagined the curtains billowing? Were my eyes playing tricks on me?

I hurried back through the strange shadows to my bed and pulled the covers up as high as they would go. "Amanda, stop scaring yourself," I scolded.

When I fell back to sleep a few minutes later, I had the ugliest, most terrifying dream.

I dreamed that we were all dead. Mom, Dad, Josh, and me.

At first, I saw us sitting around the dinner table in the new dining room. The room was very bright, so bright I couldn't see our faces very well. They were just a bright white blur.

But then, slowly, slowly, everything came into focus, and I could see that beneath our hair, we had no faces. Our skin was gone, and only our gray-green skulls were left. Bits of flesh clung to my bony cheeks. There were only deep, black sockets where my eyes had been.

The four of us, all dead, sat eating in silence. Our dinner plates, I saw, were filled with small bones. A big platter in the center of the table was piled high with gray-green bones, human-looking bones.

And then, in this dream, our disgusting meal was interrupted by a loud knocking on the door, an insistent pounding that grew louder and louder. It was Kathy, my friend from back home. I could see her at our front door, pounding on it with both fists.

I wanted to go answer the door. I wanted to run from the dining room and pull open the door and greet Kathy. I wanted to talk to Kathy. I wanted to tell her what had happened to me, to explain that I was dead and that my face had fallen away.

I wanted to see Kathy *so* badly.

But I couldn't get up from the table. I tried and tried, but I couldn't get up.

The pounding on the door grew louder and louder, until it was deafening. But I just sat there with my gruesome family, picking up bones from my dinner plate and eating them.

I woke up with a start, the horror of the dream still with me. I could still hear the pounding in my ears. I shook my head, trying to chase the dream away.

It was morning. I could tell from the blue of the sky outside the window.

"Oh, no."

The curtains. They were billowing again, flapping noisily as they blew into the room.

I sat up and stared.

The window was still closed.

"I'll take a look at the window. There must be a draft or a leak or something," Dad said at breakfast. He shoveled in another mouthful of scrambled eggs and ham.

"But, Dad — it's so weird!" I insisted, still feeling scared. "The curtains were blowing like crazy, and the window was *closed*!"

"There might be a pane missing," Dad suggested.

"Amanda is a pain!" Josh cracked. His idea of a really witty joke.

"Don't start with your sister," Mom said, putting her plate down on the table and dropping into her chair. She looked tired. Her black hair, usually carefully pulled back, was disheveled. She tugged at the belt on her bathrobe. "Whew. I don't think I slept two hours last night."

"Neither did I," I said, sighing. "I kept thinking that boy would show up in my room again."

45

"Amanda — you've really got to stop this," Mom said sharply. "Boys in your room. Curtains blowing. You have to realize that you're nervous, and your imagination is working overtime."

"But, Mom —" I started.

"Maybe a ghost was behind the curtains," Josh said, teasing. He raised up his hands and made a ghostly *oooooooh* wail.

"Whoa." Mom put a hand on Josh's shoulder. "Remember what you promised about scaring each other?"

"It's going to be hard for all of us to adjust to this place," Dad said. "You may have dreamed about the curtains blowing, Amanda. You said you had bad dreams, right?"

The terrifying nightmare flashed back into my mind. Once again I saw the big platter of bones on the table. I shivered.

"It's so damp in here," Mom said.

"A little sunshine will help dry the place out," Dad said.

I peered out the window. The sky had turned solid gray. Trees seemed to spread darkness over our backyard. "Where's Petey?" I asked.

"Out back," Mom replied, swallowing a mouthful of eggs. "He got up early, too. Couldn't sleep, I guess. So I let him out."

"What are we doing today?" Josh asked. He always needed to know the plan for the day. Every detail. Mainly so he could argue about it.

"Your father and I still have a lot of unpacking to do," Mom said, glancing to the back hallway, which was cluttered with unopened cartons. "You two can explore the neighborhood. See what you can find out. See if there are any other kids your age around."

"In other words, you want us to get lost!" I said.

Mom and Dad both laughed. "You're very smart, Amanda."

"But I want to help unpack *my* stuff," Josh whined. I knew he'd argue with the plan, just like always.

"Go get dressed and take a long walk," Dad said. "Take Petey with you, okay? And take a leash for him. I left one by the front stairs."

"What about our bikes? Why can't we ride our bikes?" Josh asked.

"They're buried in the back of the garage," Dad told him. "You'll never be able to get to them. Besides, you have a flat tire."

"If I can't ride my bike, I'm not going out," Josh insisted, crossing his arms in front of his chest.

Mom and Dad had to argue with him. Then threaten him. Finally, he agreed to go for "a short walk."

I finished breakfast, thinking about Kathy and my other friends back home. I wondered what the kids were like here in Dark Falls. I wondered if I'd be able to find new friends, real friends.

I volunteered to do the breakfast dishes since Mom and Dad had so much work to do. The warm water felt soothing on my hands as I sponged the dishes clean. I guess maybe I'm weird. I like washing dishes.

Behind me, from somewhere in the front of the house, I could hear Josh arguing with Dad. I could just barely make out the words over the trickle of the tap water.

"Your basketball is packed in one of these cartons," Dad was saying. Then Josh said something. Then Dad said, "How should *I* know which one?" Then Josh said something. Then Dad said, "No, I don't have time to look now. Believe it or not, your basketball isn't at the top of my list."

I stacked the last dish on the counter to drain and looked for a dish towel to dry my hands. There was none in sight. I guess they hadn't been unpacked yet.

Wiping off my hands on the front of my robe, I headed for the stairs. "I'll be dressed in five minutes," I called to Josh, who was still arguing with Dad in the living room. "Then we can go out."

I started up the front stairs and then stopped.

Above me on the landing stood a strange girl, about my age, with short black hair. She was smiling down at me, not a warm smile, not a friendly smile, but the coldest, most frightening smile I had ever seen.

A hand touched my shoulder.

I spun around.

It was Josh. "I'm not going for a walk unless I can take my basketball," he said.

"Josh — please!" I looked back up to the landing, and the girl was gone.

I felt cold all over. My legs were all trembly. I grabbed the banister.

"Dad! Come here — please!" I called.

Josh's face filled with alarm. "Hey, I didn't do anything!" he shouted.

"No — it's — it's not you," I said, and called Dad again.

"Amanda, I'm kind of busy," Dad said, appearing at the foot of the stairs, already perspiring from unpacking living room stuff.

"Dad, I saw somebody," I told him. "Up there. A girl." I pointed.

"Amanda, please," he replied, making a face. "Stop seeing things — okay? There's no one in this house except the four of us . . . and maybe a few mice."

"Mice?" Josh asked with sudden interest. "Really? Where?"

"Dad, I didn't imagine it," I said, my voice cracking. I was really hurt that he didn't believe me.

"Amanda, look up there," Dad said, gazing up to the landing. "What do you see?"

I followed his gaze. There was a pile of my clothes on the landing. Mom must have just unpacked them.

"It's just clothes," Dad said impatiently. "It's not a girl. It's clothes." He rolled his eyes.

"Sorry," I said quietly. I repeated it as I started up the stairs. "Sorry."

But I didn't really feel sorry. I felt confused. And still scared.

Was it possible that I thought a pile of clothes was a smiling girl?

No. I didn't think so.

I'm not crazy. And I have really good eyesight.

So then what was going on?

I opened the door to my room, turned on the ceiling light, and saw the curtains billowing in front of the bay window.

*Oh, no. Not again,* I thought.

I hurried over to them. This time, the window was open.

Who opened it?

Mom, I guessed.

Warm, wet air blew into the room. The sky was heavy and gray. It smelled like rain.

Turning to my bed, I had another shock.

Someone had laid out an outfit for me. A pair of faded jeans and a pale blue sleeveless T-shirt. They were spread out side by side at the foot of the bed.

Who had put them there? Mom?

I stood at the doorway and called to her. "Mom? Mom? Did you pick out clothes for me?"

I could hear her shout something from downstairs, but I couldn't make out the words.

*Calm down, Amanda,* I told myself. *Calm down.*

Of *course* Mom pulled the clothes out. Of *course* Mom put them there.

From the doorway, I heard whispering in my closet.

Whispering and hushed giggling behind the closet door.

This was the last straw. "What's going on here?" I yelled at the top of my lungs.

I stormed over to the closet and pulled open the door.

Frantically, I pushed clothes out of the way. No one in there.

*Mice?* I thought. *Had I heard the mice that Dad was talking about?*

"I've got to get out of here," I said aloud.

The room, I realized, was driving me crazy.

No. I was driving *myself* crazy. Imagining all of these weird things.

There was a logical explanation for everything. Everything.

As I pulled up my jeans and fastened them, I said the word *logical* over and over in my mind. I said it so many times that it didn't sound like a real word anymore.

*Calm down, Amanda. Calm down.*

I took a deep breath and held it to ten.

"Boo!"

"Josh — cut it out. You didn't scare me," I told him, sounding more cross than I had meant to.

"Let's get out of here," he said, staring at me from the doorway. "This place gives me the creeps."

"Huh? You, too?" I exclaimed. "What's *your* problem?"

He started to say something, then stopped. He suddenly looked embarrassed. "Forget it," he muttered.

"No, tell me," I insisted. "What were you going to say?"

He kicked at the floor molding. "I had a really creepy dream last night," he finally admitted, looking past me to the fluttering curtains at the window.

"A dream?" I remembered my horrible dream.

"Yeah. There were these two boys in my room. And they were mean."

"What did they do?" I asked.

"I don't remember," Josh said, avoiding my eyes. "I just remember they were scary."

"And what happened?" I asked, turning to the mirror to brush my hair.

"I woke up," he said. And then added impatiently, "Come *on*. Let's go."

"Did the boys say anything to you?" I asked.

"No. I don't think so," he answered thoughtfully. "They just laughed."

"Laughed?"

"Well, giggled, sort of," Josh said. "I don't want to talk about it anymore," he snapped. "Are we going for this dumb walk or not?"

"Okay. I'm ready," I said, putting down my brush, taking one last look in the mirror. "Let's go on this dumb walk."

I followed him down the hall. As we passed the stack of clothes on the landing, I thought about the girl I had seen standing there. And I thought about the boy in the window when we first arrived. And the two boys Josh had seen in his dream.

I decided it proved that Josh and I were both really nervous about moving to this new place. Maybe Mom and Dad were right. We were letting our imaginations run away with us.

It had to be our imaginations.

I mean, what *else* could it be?

A few seconds later, we stepped into the backyard to get Petey. He was as glad to see us as ever, leaping on us with his muddy paws, yapping excitedly, running in frantic circles through the leaves. It cheered me up just to see him.

It was hot and muggy even though the sky was gray. There was no wind at all. The heavy old trees stood as still as statues.

We headed down the gravel driveway toward the street, our sneakers kicking at the dead brown leaves, Petey running in zigzags, first in front of us, then behind. "At least Dad hasn't asked us to rake all these old leaves," Josh said.

"He will," I warned. "I don't think he's unpacked the rake yet."

Josh made a face. We stood at the curb, looking up at our house, the two second-floor bay windows staring back at us like eyes.

The house next door, I noticed for the first time, was about the same size as ours, except it was shingle instead of brick. The curtains in the living room were drawn shut. Some of the upstairs windows were shuttered. Tall trees cast the neighbors' house in darkness, too.

"Which way?" Josh asked, tossing a stick for Petey to chase.

I pointed up the street. "The school is up that way," I said. "Let's check it out."

The road sloped uphill. Josh picked up a small tree branch from the side of the road and used it as a walking stick. Petey kept trying to chew on it while Josh walked.

We didn't see anyone on the street or in any of the front yards we passed. No cars went by.

I was beginning to think the whole town was deserted, until the boy stepped out from behind a low ledge.

He popped out so suddenly, both Josh and I stopped in our tracks. "Hi," he said shyly, giving us a little wave.

"Hi," Josh and I answered at the same time.

Then, before we could pull him back, Petey ran up to the boy, sniffed his sneakers, and began snarling and barking. The boy stepped back and raised his hands as if he were protecting himself. He looked really frightened.

"Petey — stop!" I cried.

Josh grabbed the dog and picked him up, but he kept growling.

"He doesn't bite," I told the boy. "He usually doesn't bark, either. I'm sorry."

"That's okay," the boy said, staring at Petey, who was squirming to get out of Josh's arms. "He probably smells something on me."

"Petey, stop!" I shouted. The dog wouldn't stop squirming. "You don't want the leash — do you?"

The boy had short, wavy blond hair and very pale blue eyes. He had a funny turned-up nose that seemed out of place on his serious-looking face. He was wearing a maroon long-sleeve sweat-shirt, despite the mugginess of the day, and black straight-leg jeans. He had a blue baseball cap stuffed into the back pocket of his jeans.

"I'm Amanda Benson," I said. "And this is my brother, Josh."

Josh hesitantly put Petey back on the ground. The dog yipped once, stared up at the boy, whim-pered softly, then sat down on the street and began to scratch himself.

"I'm Ray Thurston," the boy said, stuffing his hands into his jeans pockets, still staring warily at Petey. He seemed to relax a little, though, see-ing that the dog had lost interest in barking and growling at him.

I suddenly realized that Ray looked familiar. Where had I seen him before? Where? I stared hard at him until I remembered.

And then I gasped in sudden fright.

Ray was the boy, the boy in my room. The boy in the window.

"You —" I stammered accusingly. "You were in our house!"

He looked confused. "Huh?"

"You were in my room — right?" I insisted.

He laughed. "I don't get it," he said. "In your room?"

Petey raised his head and gave a low growl in Ray's direction. Then he went back to his serious scratching.

"I thought I saw you," I said, beginning to feel a little doubtful. Maybe it wasn't him. Maybe . . .

"I haven't been in your house in a long time," Ray said, looking down warily at Petey.

"A long time?"

"Yeah. I used to live in your house," he replied.

"Huh?" Josh and I stared at him in surprise. "Our house?"

Ray nodded. "When we first moved here," he said. He picked up a flat pebble and heaved it down the street.

Petey growled, started to chase it, changed his mind, and plopped back down on the street, his stub of a tail wagging excitedly.

Heavy clouds lowered across the sky. It seemed to grow darker. "Where do you live now?" I asked.

Ray tossed another stone, then pointed up the road.

"Did you like our house?" Josh asked Ray.

"Yeah, it was okay," Ray told him. "Nice and shady."

"You liked it?" Josh cried. "I think it's gross. It's so dark and —"

Petey interrupted. He decided to start barking at Ray again, running up till he was a few inches in front of Ray, then backing away. Ray took a few cautious steps back to the edge of the curb.

Josh pulled the leash from the pocket of his shorts. "Sorry, Petey," he said. I held the growling dog while Josh attached the leash to his collar.

"He's never done this before. Really," I said, apologizing to Ray.

The leash seemed to confuse Petey. He tugged against it, pulling Josh across the street. But at least he stopped barking.

"Let's do something," Josh said impatiently.

"Like what?" Ray asked, relaxing again now that Petey was on the leash.

We all thought for a while.

"Maybe we could go to your house," Josh suggested to Ray.

Ray shook his head. "No. I don't think so," he said. "Not now, anyway."

"Where is everyone?" I asked, looking up and down the empty street. "It's really dead around here, huh?"

He chuckled. "Yeah. I guess you could say that," he said. "Want to go to the playground behind the school?"

"Yeah. Okay," I agreed.

The three of us headed up the street, Ray leading the way, me walking a few feet behind him, Josh holding his tree branch in one hand, the leash in the other, Petey running this way, then that, giving Josh a really hard time.

We didn't see the gang of kids till we turned the corner.

There were ten or twelve of them, mostly boys but a few girls, too. They were laughing and shouting, shoving each other playfully as they came toward us down the center of the street. Some of them, I saw, were about my age. The rest were teenagers. They were wearing jeans and dark T-shirts. One of the girls stood out because she had long, straight blond hair and was wearing green spandex tights.

"Hey, look!" a tall boy with slicked-back black hair cried, pointing at us.

Seeing Ray, Josh, and me, they grew quiet but didn't stop moving toward us. A few of them giggled, as if they were enjoying some kind of private joke.

The three of us stopped and watched them approach. I smiled and waited to say hi. Petey was pulling at his leash and barking his head off.

"Hi, guys," the tall boy with the black hair said, grinning. The others thought this was very funny for some reason. They laughed. The girl in the green tights gave a short red-haired boy a shove that almost sent him sprawling into me.

"How's it going, Ray?" a girl with short black hair asked, smiling at Ray.

"Not bad. Hi, guys," Ray answered. He turned to Josh and me. "These are some of my friends. They're all from the neighborhood."

"Hi," I said, feeling awkward. I wished Petey would stop barking and pulling at his leash like that. Poor Josh was having a terrible time holding on to him.

"This is George Carpenter," Ray said, pointing to the short red-haired boy, who nodded. "And Jerry Franklin, Karen Somerset, Bill Gregory . . ." He went around the circle, naming each kid. I tried to remember all the names but, of course, it was impossible.

"How do you like Dark Falls?" one of the girls asked me.

"I don't really know," I told her. "It's my first day here. It seems nice."

Some of the kids laughed at my answer, for some reason.

"What kind of dog is that?" George Carpenter asked Josh.

Josh, holding tight to the leash handle, told him. George stared hard at Petey, studying him, as if he had never seen a dog like Petey before.

Karen Somerset, a tall, pretty girl with short blond hair, came up to me while some of the other kids were admiring Petey. "You know, I used to live in your house," she said softly.

"What?" I wasn't sure I'd heard her correctly.

"Let's go to the playground," Ray said, interrupting.

No one responded to Ray's suggestion.

They grew quiet. Even Petey stopped barking.

Had Karen really said that she used to live in our house? I wanted to ask her, but she had stepped back into the circle of kids.

The circle.

My mouth dropped open as I realized they had formed a circle around Josh and me.

I felt a stab of fear. Was I imagining it? Was something going on?

They all suddenly looked different to me. They were smiling, but their faces were tense, watchful, as if they expected trouble.

Two of them, I noticed, were carrying baseball bats. The girl with the green tights stared at me, looking me up and down, checking me out.

No one said a word. The street was silent except for Petey, who was now whimpering softly.

I suddenly felt very afraid.

Why were they staring at us like that?

Or was my imagination running away with me again?

I turned to Ray, who was still beside me. He didn't seem at all troubled. But he didn't return my gaze.

"Hey, guys —" I said. "What's going on?" I tried to keep it light, but my voice was a little shaky.

I looked over at Josh. He was busy soothing Petey and hadn't noticed that things had changed.

The two boys with baseball bats held them up waist high and moved forward.

I glanced around the circle, feeling the fear tighten my chest.

The circle tightened. The kids were closing in on us.

The black clouds overhead seemed to lower. The air felt heavy and damp.

Josh was fussing with Petey's collar and still didn't see what was happening. I wondered if Ray was going to say anything, if he was going to do anything to stop them. But he stayed frozen and expressionless beside me.

The circle grew smaller as the kids closed in.

I realized I'd been holding my breath. I took a deep breath and opened my mouth to cry out.

"Hey, kids — what's going on?"

It was a man's voice, calling from outside the circle.

Everyone turned to see Mr. Dawes coming quickly toward us, taking long strides as he crossed the street, his open blazer flapping behind him. He had a friendly smile on his face. "What's going on?" he asked again.

He didn't seem to realize that the gang of kids had been closing in on Josh and me.

"We're heading to the playground," George Carpenter told him, twirling the bat in his hand. "You know. To play softball."

"Good deal," Mr. Dawes said, pulling down his striped tie, which had blown over his shoulder. He looked up at the darkening sky. "Hope you don't get rained out."

Several of the kids had backed up. They were standing in small groups of two and three now. The circle had completely broken up.

"Is that bat for softball or hardball?" Mr. Dawes asked George.

"George doesn't know," another kid replied quickly. "He's never hit anything with it!"

The kids all laughed. George playfully menaced the kid, pretending to come at him with the bat.

Mr. Dawes gave a little wave and started to leave. But then he stopped, and his eyes opened wide with surprise. "Hey," he said, flashing me a friendly smile. "Josh. Amanda. I didn't see you there."

"Good morning," I muttered. I was feeling very confused. A moment ago, I'd felt terribly scared. Now everyone was laughing and kidding around.

Had I imagined that the kids were moving in on us? Ray and Josh hadn't seemed to notice anything peculiar. Was it just me and my overactive imagination?

What would have happened if Mr. Dawes hadn't come along?

"How are you two getting along in the new house?" Mr. Dawes asked, smoothing back his wavy blond hair.

"Okay," Josh and I answered together. Looking up at Mr. Dawes, Petey began to bark and pull at the leash.

Mr. Dawes put an exaggerated hurt expression on his face. "I'm crushed," he said. "Your dog still doesn't like me." He bent over Petey. "Hey, dog — lighten up."

Petey barked back angrily.

"He doesn't seem to like *anybody* today," I told Mr. Dawes apologetically.

Mr. Dawes stood back up and shrugged. "Can't win 'em all." He started back to his car, parked a few yards down the street. "I'm heading over to your house," he told Josh and me. "Just want to see if there's anything I can do to help your parents. Have fun, kids."

I watched him climb into his car and drive away.

"He's a nice guy," Ray said.

"Yeah," I agreed. I was still feeling uncomfortable, wondering what the kids would do now that Mr. Dawes was gone.

Would they form that frightening circle again?

No. Everyone started walking, heading down the block to the playground behind the school. They were kidding each other and talking normally, and pretty much ignored Josh and me.

I was starting to feel a little silly. It was obvious that they hadn't been trying to scare Josh and me. I must have made the whole thing up in my mind.

I must have.

*At least*, I told myself, *I didn't scream or make a scene. At least I didn't make a total fool of myself.*

The playground was completely empty. I guessed that most kids had stayed inside because of the threatening sky. The playground was a large, flat grassy field, surrounded on all four sides by a tall metal fence. There were swings and slides at the end nearest the school building. There were two baseball diamonds on the other end. Beyond the fence, I could see a row of tennis courts, also deserted.

Josh tied Petey to the fence, then came running over to join the rest of us. The boy named Jerry Franklin made up the teams. Ray and I were on the same team. Josh was on the other.

As our team took the field, I felt excited and a little nervous. I'm not the best softball player in the world. I can hit the ball pretty well. But in the field, I'm a complete klutz. Luckily, Jerry sent me out to right field, where not many balls are hit.

The clouds began to part a little and the sky got lighter. We played two full innings. The other team was winning, eight to two. I was having fun. I had only messed up on one play. And I hit a double my first time at bat.

It was fun being with a whole new group of kids. They seemed really nice, especially the girl named Karen Somerset, who talked with me while we waited for our turn at bat. Karen had a great smile, even though she wore braces on all her teeth, up and down. She seemed very eager to be friends.

The sun was coming out as my team started to take the field for the beginning of the third inning. Suddenly, I heard a loud, shrill whistle. I looked around until I saw that it was Jerry Franklin, blowing a silver whistle.

Everyone came running up to him. "We'd better quit," he said, looking up at the brightening sky. "We promised our folks, remember, that we'd be home for lunch."

I glanced at my watch. It was only eleven-thirty. Still early.

But to my surprise, no one protested.

They all waved to each other and called out farewells, and then began to run. I couldn't believe how fast everyone left. It was as if they were racing or something.

Karen ran past me like the others, her head down, a serious expression on her pretty face.

Then she stopped suddenly and turned around. "Nice meeting you, Amanda," she called back. "We should get together sometime."

"Great!" I called to her. "Do you know where I live?"

I couldn't hear her answer very well. She nodded, and I thought she said, "Yes. I know it. I used to live in your house."

But that *couldn't* have been what she said.

Several days went by. Josh and I were getting used to our new house and our new friends.

The kids we met every day at the playground weren't exactly friends yet. They talked with Josh and me and let us on their teams. But it was really hard to get to know them.

In my room, I kept hearing whispers late at night and soft giggling, but I forced myself to ignore it. One night, I thought I saw a girl dressed all in white at the end of the upstairs hall. But when I walked over to investigate, there was just a pile of dirty sheets and other bedclothes against the wall.

Josh and I were adjusting, but Petey was still acting really strange. We took him with us to the playground every day, but we had to leash him to the fence. Otherwise, he'd bark and snap at the kids.

"He's still nervous being in a new place," I told Josh. "He'll calm down."

But Petey didn't calm down. And about two weeks later, we were finishing up a softball game with Ray, and Karen Somerset, and Jerry Franklin, and George Carpenter, and a bunch of other kids, when I looked over to the fence and saw that Petey was gone.

Somehow he had broken out of his leash and run away.

We looked for hours, calling "Petey!" wandering from block to block, searching front yards and backyards, empty lots and woods. Then, after circling the neighborhood twice, Josh and I suddenly realized we had no idea where we were.

The streets of Dark Falls looked the same. They were all lined with sprawling old brick or shingle houses, all filled with shady old trees.

"I don't believe it. We're lost," Josh said, leaning against a tree trunk, trying to catch his breath.

"That stupid dog," I muttered, my eyes searching up the street. "Why did he do this? He's never run away before."

"I don't know how he got loose," Josh said, shaking his head, then wiping his sweaty forehead with the sleeve of his T-shirt. "I tied him up really well."

"Hey — maybe he ran home," I said. The idea immediately cheered me up.

"Yeah!" Josh stepped away from the tree and headed back over to me. "I'll bet you're right,

Amanda. He's probably been home for hours. Wow. We've been stupid. We should've checked home first. Let's go!"

"Well," I said, looking around at the empty yards, "we just have to figure out which way is home."

I looked up and down the street, trying to figure out which way we'd turned when we left the school playground. I couldn't remember, so we just started walking.

Luckily, as we reached the next corner, the school came into sight. We had made a full circle. It was easy to find our way from there.

Passing the playground, I stared at the spot on the fence where Petey had been tied. That troublemaking dog. He'd been acting so badly ever since we came to Dark Falls.

Would he be home when we got there? I hoped so.

A few minutes later, Josh and I were running up the gravel driveway, calling the dog's name at the top of our lungs. The front door burst open and Mom, her hair tied in a red bandanna, the knees of her jeans covered with dust, leaned out. She and Dad had been painting the back porch. "Where have you two been? Lunchtime was two hours ago!"

Josh and I both answered at the same time. "Is Petey here?"

"We've been looking for Petey!"

"Is he here?"

Mom's face filled with confusion. "Petey? I thought he was with you."

My heart sank. Josh slumped to the driveway with a loud sigh, sprawling flat on his back in the gravel and leaves.

"You haven't seen him?" I asked, my trembling voice showing my disappointment. "He *was* with us. But he ran away."

"Oh. I'm sorry," Mom said, motioning for Josh to get up from the driveway. "He ran away? I thought you've been keeping him on a leash."

"You've got to help us find him," Josh pleaded, not budging from the ground. "Get the car. We've got to find him — right now!"

"I'm sure he hasn't gotten far," Mom said. "You must be starving. Come in and have some lunch and then we'll —"

"No. Right *now*!" Josh screamed.

"What's going on?" Dad, his face and hair covered with tiny flecks of white paint, joined Mom on the front porch. "Josh — what's all the yelling?"

We explained to Dad what had happened. He said he was too busy to drive around looking for Petey. Mom said she'd do it, but only after we had some lunch. I pulled Josh up by both arms and dragged him into the house.

We washed up and gulped down some peanut butter and jelly sandwiches. Then Mom took the car out of the garage, and we drove around and around the neighborhood searching for our lost pet.

With no luck.

No sign of him.

Josh and I were miserable. Heartbroken. Mom and Dad called the local police. Dad kept saying that Petey had a good sense of direction, that he'd show up any minute.

But we didn't really believe it.

Where was he?

The four of us ate dinner in silence. It was the longest, most horrible evening of my life. "I tied him up really good," Josh repeated, close to tears, his dinner plate still full.

"Dogs are great escape artists," Dad said. "Don't worry. He'll show up."

"Some night for a party," Mom said glumly.

I'd completely forgotten that they were going out. Some neighbors on the next block had invited them to a big party.

"I sure don't feel like partying, either," Dad said with a sigh. "I'm beat from painting all day. But I guess we have to be neighborly. Sure you kids will be okay here?"

"Yeah, I guess," I said, thinking about Petey. I kept listening for his bark, listening for scratching at the door.

But no. The hours dragged by. Petey still hadn't shown up by bedtime.

Josh and I both slinked upstairs. I felt really tired, weary from all the worrying, and the running around and searching for Petey, I guess. But I knew I'd never be able to get to sleep.

In the hall outside my bedroom door, I heard whispering from inside my room and quiet footsteps. The usual sounds my room made. I wasn't at all scared of them or surprised by them anymore.

Without hesitating, I stepped into my room and clicked on the light. The room was empty, as I knew it would be. The mysterious sounds disappeared. I glanced at the curtains, which lay straight and still.

Then I saw the clothes strewn all over my bed.

Several pairs of jeans. Several T-shirts. A couple of sweatshirts. My only dress-up skirt.

*That's strange*, I thought. Mom was such a neat freak. If she had washed these things, she surely would have hung them up or put them into dresser drawers.

Sighing wearily, I started to gather up the clothes and put them away. I figured that Mom simply had too much to do to be bothered. She had probably washed the stuff and then left it here for me to put away. Or she had put it all down, planning to come back later and put it away, and then got busy with other chores.

Half an hour later, I was tucked into my bed, wide awake, staring at the shadows on the ceiling. Some time after that — I lost track of the time — I was still wide awake, still thinking about Petey, thinking about the new kids I'd met, thinking about the new neighborhood, when I heard my bedroom door creak and swing open.

Footsteps on the creaking floorboards.

I sat up in the darkness as someone crept into my room.

"Amanda — *shhh* — it's me."

Alarmed, it took me a few seconds to recognize the hushed whisper. "Josh! What do you want? What are you doing in here?"

I gasped as a blinding light forced me to cover my eyes. "Oops. Sorry," Josh said. "My flashlight. I didn't mean to —"

"Ow, that's bright," I said, blinking. He aimed the powerful beam of white light up at the ceiling.

"Yeah. It's a halogen flashlight," he said.

"Well, what do you want?" I asked irritably. I still couldn't see well. I rubbed my eyes, but it didn't help.

"I know where Petey is," Josh whispered, "and I'm going to go get him. Come with me?"

"Huh?" I looked at the little clock on my bed table. "It's after midnight, Josh."

"So? It won't take long. Really."

My eyes were nearly normal by now. Staring at Josh in the light from the halogen flashlight, I noticed for the first time that he was fully dressed in jeans and a long-sleeve T-shirt.

"I don't get it, Josh," I said, swinging around and putting my feet on the floor. "We looked everywhere. Where do you think Petey is?"

"In the cemetery," Josh answered. His eyes looked big and dark and serious in the white light.

"Huh?"

"That's where he ran the first time, remember? When we first came to Dark Falls? He ran to that cemetery just past the school."

"Now, wait a minute —" I started.

"We drove past it this afternoon, but we didn't look inside. He's there, Amanda. I know he is. And I'm going to go get him whether you come or not."

"Josh, calm down," I said, putting my hands on his narrow shoulders. I was surprised to discover that he was trembling. "There's no reason for Petey to be in that cemetery."

"That's where he went the first time," Josh insisted. "He was looking for something there that day. I could tell. I know he's there again, Amanda." He pulled away from me. "Are you coming or not?"

My brother has to be the stubbornest, most headstrong person in the world.

76

"Josh, you're really going to walk into a strange cemetery so late at night?" I asked.

"I'm not afraid," he said, shining the bright light around my room.

For a brief second, I thought the light caught someone, lurking behind the curtains. I opened my mouth to cry out. But there was no one there.

"You coming or not?" he repeated impatiently.

I was going to say no. But then, glancing at the curtains, I thought, *It's probably no more spooky out there in that cemetery than it is here in my own bedroom!*

"Yeah. Okay," I said grudgingly. "Get out of here and let me get dressed."

"Okay," he whispered, turning off the flashlight, plunging us into blackness. "Meet me down at the end of the driveway."

"Josh — one quick look at the cemetery, then we hurry home. Got it?" I told him.

"Yeah. Right. We'll be home before Mom and Dad get back from that party." He crept out. I could hear him making his way quickly down the stairs.

*This is the craziest idea ever,* I told myself as I searched in the darkness for some clothes to pull on.

And it was also kind of exciting.

Josh was wrong. No doubt about it. Petey wouldn't be hanging around in that cemetery now. Why on earth should he?

But at least it wasn't a long walk. And it was an adventure. Something to write about to Kathy back home.

And if Josh happened to be right, and we did manage to find poor, lost Petey, well, that would be great, too.

A few minutes later, dressed in jeans and a sweatshirt, I crept out of the house and joined Josh at the bottom of the driveway. The night was still warm. A heavy blanket of clouds covered the moon. I realized for the first time that there were no streetlights on our block.

Josh had the halogen flashlight on, aimed down at our feet. "You ready?" he asked.

Dumb question. Would I be standing there if I weren't ready?

We crunched over dead leaves as we headed up the block, toward the school. From there, it was just two blocks to the cemetery.

"It's so dark," I whispered. The houses were black and silent. There was no breeze at all. It was as if we were all alone in the world.

"It's too quiet," I said, hurrying to keep up with Josh. "No crickets or anything. Are you sure you really want to go to the cemetery?"

"I'm sure," he said, his eyes following the circle of light from the flashlight as it bumped over the ground. "I really think Petey is there."

We walked in the street, keeping close to the curb. We had gone nearly two blocks. The school was just coming into sight on the next block when we heard the scraping steps behind us on the pavement.

Josh and I both stopped. He lowered the light.

We both heard the sounds. I wasn't imagining them.

Someone was following us.

Josh was so startled, the flashlight tumbled from his hand and clattered onto the street. The light flickered but didn't go out.

By the time Josh had managed to pick it up, our pursuer had caught up to us. I spun around to face him, my heart pounding in my chest.

"Ray! What are *you* doing here?"

Josh aimed the light at Ray's face, but Ray shot his arms up to shield his face and ducked back into the darkness. "What are *you two* doing here?" he cried, sounding almost as startled as I did.

"You — you scared us," Josh said angrily, aiming the flashlight back down at our feet.

"Sorry," Ray said. "I would've called out, but I wasn't sure it was you."

"Josh has this crazy idea about where Petey might be," I told him, still struggling to catch my breath. "That's why we're out here."

"What about you?" Josh asked Ray.

"Well, sometimes I have troubling sleeping," Ray said softly.

"Don't your parents mind you being out so late?" I asked.

In the glow from the flashlight, I could see a wicked smile cross his face. "They don't know."

"Are we going to the cemetery or not?" Josh asked impatiently. Without waiting for an answer, he started jogging up the road, the light bobbing on the pavement in front of him. I turned and followed, wanting to stay close to the light.

"Where are you going?" Ray called, hurrying to catch up.

"The cemetery," I called back.

"No," Ray said. "You're not."

His voice was so low, so threatening, that I stopped. "What?"

"You're not going there," Ray repeated. I couldn't see his face. It was hidden in darkness. But his words sounded menacing.

"Hurry!" Josh called back to us. He hadn't slowed down. He didn't seem to notice the threat in Ray's words.

"Stop, Josh!" Ray called. It sounded more like an order than a request. "You can't go there!"

"Why not?" I demanded, suddenly afraid. Was Ray threatening Josh and me? Did he know something we didn't? Or was I making a big deal out of nothing once again?

I stared into the darkness, trying to see his face.

"You'd be nuts to go there at night!" he declared.

I began to think I had misjudged him. He was afraid to go there. That's why he was trying to stop us.

"Are you coming or not?" Josh demanded, getting farther and farther ahead of us.

"I don't think we should," Ray warned.

*Yes, he's afraid,* I decided. I only imagined that he was threatening us.

"You don't have to. But *we* do," Josh insisted, picking up his speed.

"No. Really," Ray said. "This is a bad idea." But now he and I were running side by side to catch up with Josh.

"Petey's there," Josh said. "I know he is."

We passed the dark, silent school. It seemed much bigger at night. Josh's light flashed through the low tree branches as we turned the corner onto Cemetery Drive.

"Wait — please," Ray pleaded. But Josh didn't slow down. Neither did I. I was eager to get there and get it over with.

I wiped my forehead with my sleeve. The air was hot and still. I wished I hadn't worn a sweatshirt. I felt my hair. It was dripping wet.

The clouds still covered the moon as we reached the cemetery. We stepped through a gate in the low wall. In the darkness, I could see the crooked rows of gravestones.

Josh's light traveled from stone to stone, jumping up and down as he walked. "Petey!" he called suddenly, interrupting the silence.

*He's disturbing the sleep of the dead,* I thought, feeling a sudden chill of fear.

*Don't be silly, Amanda.* "Petey!" I called, too, forcing away my morbid thoughts.

"This is a very bad idea," Ray said, standing very close to me.

"Petey! Petey!" Josh called.

"I know it's a bad idea," I admitted to Ray. "But I didn't want Josh to come here by himself."

"But we shouldn't *be* here," Ray insisted.

I was beginning to wish he'd go away. No one had forced him to come. Why was he giving us such a hard time?

"Hey — look at this!" Josh called from several yards up ahead.

My sneakers crunching over the soft ground, I hurried between the rows of graves. I hadn't realized that we had already walked the entire length of the graveyard.

"Look," Josh said again, his flashlight playing over a strange structure built at the edge of the cemetery.

It took me a little while to figure out what it was in the small circle of light. It was so unexpected. It was some kind of theater. An amphitheater, I guess you'd call it, circular rows of bench seats dug into the ground, descending like stairs to a low stagelike platform at the bottom.

"What on earth?" I exclaimed.

I started forward to get a closer look.

"Amanda — wait. Let's go home," Ray called. He grabbed at my arm, but I hurried away, and he grabbed only air.

"Weird! Who would build an outdoor theater at the edge of a cemetery?" I asked.

I looked back to see if Josh and Ray were following me, and my sneaker caught against something. I stumbled to the ground, hitting my knee hard.

"Ow. What was that?"

Josh shone the light on it as I climbed slowly, painfully, to my feet. I had tripped over an enormous upraised tree root.

In the flickering light, I followed the gnarled root over to a wide old tree several yards away. The huge tree was bent over the strange below-ground theater, leaning at such a low angle that it looked likely to topple over at any second. Big clumps of roots were raised up from the ground. Overhead, the tree's branches, heavy with leaves, seemed to lean to the ground.

"Timberrr!" Josh yelled.

"How weird!" I exclaimed. "Hey, Ray — what is this place?"

"It's a meeting place," Ray said quietly, standing close beside me, staring straight ahead at the leaning tree. "They use it sort of like a town hall. They have town meetings here."

"In the cemetery?" I cried, finding it hard to believe.

"Let's go," Ray urged, looking very nervous.

All three of us heard the footsteps. They were behind us, somewhere in the rows of graves. We turned around. Josh's light swept over the ground.

"Petey!"

There he was, standing between the nearest row of low stone grave markers. I turned happily to Josh. "I don't believe it!" I cried. "You were right!"

"Petey! Petey!" Josh and I both started running toward our dog.

But Petey arched back on his hind legs as if he were getting ready to run away. He stared at us, his eyes red as jewels in the light of the flashlight.

"Petey! We found you!" I cried.

The dog lowered his head and started to trot away.

"Petey! Hey — come back! Don't you recognize us?"

With a burst of speed, Josh caught up with him and grabbed him up off the ground. "Hey, Petey, what's the matter, fella?"

As I hurried over, Josh dropped Petey back to the ground and stepped back. "Ooh — he stinks!"

"What?" I cried.

"Petey — he stinks. He smells like a dead rat!" Josh held his nose.

Petey started to walk slowly away.

"Josh, he isn't glad to see us," I wailed. "He doesn't even seem to recognize us. Look at him!"

It was true. Petey walked to the next row of gravestones, then turned and glared at us.

I suddenly felt sick. What had happened to Petey? Why was he acting so differently? Why wasn't he glad to see us?

"I don't get it," Josh said, still making a face from the odor the dog gave off. "Usually, if we leave the room for thirty seconds, he goes nuts when we come back."

"We'd better go!" Ray called. He was still at the edge of the cemetery near the leaning tree.

"Petey — what's wrong with you?" I called to the dog. He didn't respond. "Don't you remember your name? Petey? Petey?"

"Yuck! What a stink!" Josh exclaimed.

"We've got to get him home and give him a bath," I said. My voice was shaking. I felt really sad. And frightened.

"Maybe this isn't Petey," Josh said thoughtfully. The dog's eyes again glared red in the beam of light.

"It's him, all right," I said quietly. "Look. He's dragging the leash. Go get him, Josh — and let's go home."

"*You* get him!" Josh cried. "He smells too bad!"

"Just grab his leash. You don't have to pick him up," he said.

"No. *You*."

Josh was being stubborn again. I could see that I had no choice. "Okay," I said. "I'll get him. But I'll need the light." I grabbed the flashlight from Josh's hand and started to run toward Petey.

"Sit, Petey. Sit!" I ordered. It was the only command Petey ever obeyed.

But he didn't obey it this time. Instead, he turned and trotted away, holding his head down low.

"Petey — stop! Petey, come on!" I yelled, exasperated. "Don't make me chase you."

"Don't let him get away!" Josh yelled, running up behind me.

I moved the flashlight from side to side along the ground. "Where is he?"

"Petey! Petey!" Josh called, sounding shrill and desperate.

I couldn't see him.

"Oh, no. Don't tell me we've lost him again!" I said.

We both started to call him. "What's *wrong* with that mutt?" I cried.

I moved the beam of light down one long row of gravestones, then, moving quickly, down the next. No sign of him. We both kept calling his name.

And then the circle of light came to rest on the front of the granite tombstone.

Reading the name on the stone, I stopped short.

And gasped.

"Josh — look!" I grabbed Josh's sleeve. I held on tight.

"Huh? What's wrong?" His face filled with confusion.

"Look! The name on the gravestone."

It was Karen Somerset.

Josh read the name. He stared at me, still confused.

"That's my new friend, Karen. The one I talk to on the playground every day," I said.

"Huh? It must be her grandmother or something," Josh said, and then added impatiently, "Come on. Look for Petey."

"No. Look at the dates," I said to him.

We both read the dates under Karen Somerset's name. 1977–1989.

"It can't be her mother or grandmother," I said, keeping the beam of light on the stone despite my trembling hand. "This girl died when she was twelve. My age. And Karen is twelve, too. She told me."

"Amanda —" Josh scowled and looked away.

But I took a few steps and beamed the light onto the next gravestone. There was a name on it I'd never heard before. I moved on to the next stone. Another name I'd never heard.

"Amanda, come on!" Josh whined.

The next gravestone had the name George Carpenter on it. 1991–2004.

"Josh — look! It's George from the playground," I called.

"Amanda, we have to get Petey," he insisted, grabbing the flashlight from me.

But I couldn't pull myself away from the gravestones. I went from one to the next, trying to read the names in the darkness.

To my growing horror, I found Jerry Franklin. And then Bill Gregory.

All the kids we had played softball with. They all had gravestones here.

My heart thudding, I moved down the crooked row, my sneakers sinking into the soft grass. I felt numb, numb with fear. I struggled to see the writing on the last stone in the row.

RAY THURSTON. 1993–2004.

"Huh?"

I could hear Josh calling me, but I couldn't make out what he was saying.

The rest of the world seemed to fall away. I read the deeply etched inscription again:

RAY THURSTON. 1993–2004.

I stood there, staring at the letters and numbers. I stared at them till they didn't make sense anymore, until they were just a gray blur.

Suddenly, I realized that Ray had crept up beside the gravestone and was staring at me.

"Ray —" I managed to say, looking at the name on the stone. "Ray, this one is . . . *you!*"

His eyes flared, glowing like dying embers.

"Yes, it's me," he said softly, moving toward me. "I'm so sorry, Amanda."

I took a step back, my sneakers sinking into the soft ground. The air was heavy and still. No one made a sound. Nothing moved.

Dead.

*I'm surrounded by death*, I thought.

Then, frozen to the spot, unable to breathe, the darkness swirling around me, the gravestones spinning in their own black shadows, I thought: *What is he going to do to me?*

"Ray —" I managed to call out. My voice sounded faint and far away. "Ray, are you really dead?"

"I'm sorry. You weren't supposed to find out yet," he said, his voice floating low and heavy on the stifling night air.

"But — how? I mean . . . I don't understand. . . ." I looked past him to the darting white light of the flashlight. Josh was several rows away, almost to the street, still searching for Petey.

"Petey!" I whispered, dread choking my throat, my stomach tightening in horror.

"Dogs always know," Ray said in a low, flat tone. "Dogs always recognize the living dead. That's why they have to go first. They always know."

"You mean — Petey's . . . dead?" I choked out the words.

Ray nodded. "They kill the dogs first."

"No!" I screamed and took another step back, nearly losing my balance as I bumped into a low marble gravestone. I jumped away from it.

"You weren't supposed to see this," Ray said, his narrow face expressionless except for his pale eyes, which revealed real sadness. "You weren't supposed to know. Not for another few weeks, anyway. I'm the watcher. I was supposed to watch, to make sure you didn't see until it was time."

He took a step toward me, his eyes lighting up red, burning into mine.

"Were you watching me from the window?" I cried. "Was that you in my room?"

Again he nodded yes. "I used to live in your house," he said, taking another step closer, forcing me back against the cold marble stone. "I'm the watcher."

I forced myself to look away, to stop staring into his glowing eyes. I wanted to scream to Josh to run and get help. But he was too far away. And I was frozen there, frozen with fear.

"We need fresh blood," Ray said.

"What?" I cried. "What are you saying?"

"The town — it can't survive without fresh blood. None of us can. You'll understand soon, Amanda. You'll understand why we had to invite you to the house, to the . . . Dead House."

In the darting, zigzagging beam of light, I could see Josh moving closer, heading our way.

*Run, Josh*, I thought. *Run away. Fast. Get someone. Get* anyone.

I could think the words. Why couldn't I scream them?

Ray's eyes glowed brighter. He was standing right in front of me now, his features set, hard and cold.

"Ray?" Even through my jeans, the marble gravestone felt cold against the back of my legs.

"I messed up," he whispered. "I was the watcher. But I messed up."

"Ray — what are you going to do?"

His red eyes flickered. "I'm really sorry."

He started to raise himself off the ground, to float over me.

I could feel myself start to choke. I couldn't breathe. I couldn't move. I opened my mouth to call out to Josh, but no sound came out.

Josh? Where was he?

I looked down the rows of gravestones but couldn't see his light.

Ray floated up a little higher. He hovered over me, choking me somehow, blinding me, suffocating me.

*I'm dead,* I thought. *Dead.*

*Now I'm dead, too.*

And then, suddenly, light broke through the darkness.

The light shone in Ray's face, the bright white halogen light.

"What's going on?" Josh asked, in a high-pitched, nervous voice. "Amanda — what's happening?"

Ray cried out and dropped back to the ground. "Turn that off! Turn it off!" he screeched, his voice a shrill whisper, like wind through a broken windowpane.

But Josh held the bright beam of light on Ray. "What's going on? What are you doing?"

I could breathe again. As I stared into the light, I struggled to stop my heart from pounding so hard.

Ray moved his arms to shield himself from the light. But I could see what was happening to him. The light had already done its damage.

Ray's skin seemed to be melting. His whole face sagged, then fell, dropping off his skull.

I stared into the circle of white light, unable to look away, as Ray's skin folded and drooped and melted away. As the bone underneath was revealed, his eyeballs rolled out of their sockets and fell silently to the ground.

Josh, frozen in horror, somehow held the bright light steady, and we both stared at the grinning skull, its dark craters staring back at us.

"Oh!" I shrieked as Ray took a step toward me.

But then I realized that Ray wasn't walking. He was falling.

I jumped aside as he crumpled to the ground. And gasped as his skull hit the top of the marble gravestone and cracked open with a sickening *splat*.

"Come on!" Josh shouted. "Amanda — come on!" He grabbed my hand and tried to pull me away.

But I couldn't stop staring down at Ray, now a pile of bones inside a puddle of crumpled clothes.

"Amanda, come on!"

Then, before I even realized it, I was running, running beside Josh as fast as I could down the long row of graves toward the street. The light flashed against the blur of gravestones as we ran, slipping on the soft, dew-covered grass, gasping in the still, hot air.

"We've got to tell Mom and Dad. Got to get *away* from here!" I cried.

96

"They — they won't believe it!" Josh said, as we reached the street. We kept running, our sneakers thudding hard against the pavement. "I'm not sure I believe it myself!"

"They've *got* to believe us!" I told him. "If they don't, we'll *drag* them out of the house."

The white beam of light pointed the way as we ran through the dark, silent streets. There were no streetlights, no lights on in the windows of the houses we passed, no car headlights.

Such a dark world we had entered.

And now it was time to get out.

We ran the rest of the way home. I kept looking back to see if we were being followed. But I didn't see anyone. The neighborhood was still and empty.

I had a sharp pain in my side as we reached home. But I forced myself to keep running, up the gravel driveway with its thick blanket of dead leaves and onto the front porch.

I pushed open the door and both Josh and I started to scream. "Mom! Dad! Where are you?"

Silence.

We ran into the living room. The lights were all off.

"Mom? Dad? Are you here?"

*Please be here*, I thought, my heart racing, the pain in my side still sharp. *Please be here*.

We searched the house. They weren't home.

"The party," Josh suddenly remembered. "Can they still be at that party?"

We were standing in the living room, both of us breathing hard. The pain in my side had let up just a bit. I had turned on all the lights, but the room still felt gloomy and menacing.

I glanced at the clock on the mantel. Nearly two in the morning.

"They should be home by now," I said, my voice shaky and weak.

"Where did they go? Did they leave a number?" Josh was already on his way to the kitchen.

I followed him, turning on lights as we went. We went right to the memo pad on the counter where Mom and Dad always leave us notes.

Nothing. The pad was blank.

"We've *got* to find them!" Josh cried. He sounded very frightened. His wide eyes reflected his fear. "We have to get away from here."

*What if something has happened to them?*

That's what I started to say. But I caught myself just in time. I didn't want to scare Josh any more than he was already.

Besides, he'd probably thought of that, too.

"Should we call the police?" he asked as we walked back to the living room and peered out the front window into the darkness.

"I don't know," I said, pressing my hot forehead against the cool glass. "I just don't know *what* to do. I want them to be home. I want them here so we can all leave."

"What's your hurry?" a girl's voice said from behind me.

Josh and I both cried out and spun around.

Karen Somerset was standing in the center of the room, her arms crossed over her chest.

"But — you're *dead!*" I blurted out.

She smiled, a sad smile, a bitter smile.

And then two more kids stepped in from the hallway. One of them clicked off the lights. "Too bright in here," he said. They moved next to Karen.

Then another dead kid, Jerry Franklin, appeared by the fireplace. And I saw the girl with short black hair, the one I had seen on the stairs, move beside me by the curtains.

They were all smiling, their eyes glowing dully in the dim light, all moving in on Josh and me.

"What do you *want?*" I screamed in a voice I didn't even recognize. "What are you going to do?"

"We used to live in your house," Karen said softly.

"Huh?" I cried.

"We used to live in your house," George said.

"And now, guess what?" Jerry added. *"Now we're dead in your house!"*

The others started to laugh, crackling, dry laughs, as they all closed in on Josh and me.

"They're going to kill us!" Josh cried.

I watched them move forward in silence. Josh and I had backed up to the window. I looked around the dark room for an escape route.

But there was nowhere to run.

"Karen — you seemed so nice," I said. The words just tumbled out. I hadn't thought before I said them.

Her eyes glowed a little brighter. "I *was* nice," she said in a glum monotone, "until I moved here."

"We were all nice," George Carpenter said in the same low monotone. "But now we're dead."

"Let us go!" Josh cried, raising his hands in front of him as if to shield himself. "Please — let us go."

They laughed again, the dry, hoarse laughter. Dead laughter.

"Don't be scared, Amanda," Karen said. "Soon you'll be with us. That's why they invited you to this house."

"Huh? I don't understand," I cried, my voice shaking.

"This is the Dead House. This is where everyone lives when they first arrive in Dark Falls. When they're still alive."

This seemed to strike the others as funny. They all snickered and laughed.

"But our great-uncle —" Josh started.

Karen shook her head, her eyes glowing with amusement. "No. Sorry, Josh. No great-uncle. It was just a trick to bring you here. Once every year, someone new has to move here. Other years, it was us. We lived in this house — until we died. This year, it's your turn."

"We need new blood," Jerry Franklin said, his eyes glowing red in the dim light. "Once a year, you see, we need new blood."

Moving forward in silence, they hovered over Josh and me.

I took a deep breath. A last breath, perhaps. And shut my eyes.

And then I heard the knock on the door.

A loud knock, repeated several times.

I opened my eyes. The ghostly kids all vanished.

The air smelled sour.

Josh and I stared at each other, dazed, as the loud knocking started again.

"It's Mom and Dad!" Josh cried.

We both ran to the door. Josh stumbled over the coffee table in the dark, so I got to the door first.

"Mom! Dad!" I cried, pulling open the door. "Where have you been?"

I reached out my arms to hug them both — and stopped with my arms in the air. My mouth dropped open and I uttered a silent cry.

"Mr. Dawes!" Josh exclaimed, coming up beside me. "We thought —"

"Oh, Mr. Dawes, I'm so glad to see you!" I cried happily, pushing open the screen door for him.

"Kids — you're okay?" he asked, eyeing us both, his handsome face tight with worry. "Oh, thank God!" he cried. "I got here in time!"

"Mr. Dawes —" I started, feeling so relieved, I had tears in my eyes. "I —"

He grabbed my arm. "There's no time to talk," he said, looking behind him to the street. I could see his car in the driveway. The engine was running. Only the parking lights were on. "I've got to get you kids out of here while there's still time."

Josh and I started to follow him, then hesitated.

What if Mr. Dawes was one of them?

"Hurry," Mr. Dawes urged, holding open the screen door, gazing nervously out into the darkness. "I think we're in terrible danger."

"But —" I started, staring into his frightened eyes, trying to decide if we could trust him.

"I was at the party with your parents," Mr. Dawes said. "All of a sudden, they formed a circle. Everyone. Around your parents and me. They — they started to close in on us."

*Just like when the kids started to close in on Josh and me*, I thought.

"We broke through them and ran," Mr. Dawes said, glancing to the driveway behind him. "Somehow the three of us got away. Hurry. We've all got to get away from here — *now!*"

"Josh, let's go," I urged. Then I turned to Mr. Dawes. "Where are Mom and Dad?"

"Come on. I'll show you. They're safe for now. But I don't know for how long."

We followed him out of the house and down the driveway to his car. The clouds had parted. A sliver of moon shone low in a pale early morning sky.

"There's something wrong with this whole town," Mr. Dawes said, holding the front passenger door open for me as Josh climbed into the back.

I slumped gratefully into the seat, and he slammed the door shut. "I know," I said, as he slid behind the wheel. "Josh and I. We both —"

"We've got to get as far away as we can before they catch up with us," Mr. Dawes said, backing down the drive quickly, the tires sliding and squealing as he pulled onto the street.

"Yes," I agreed. "Thank goodness you came. My house — it's filled with kids. Dead kids and —"

"So you've seen them," Mr. Dawes said softly, his eyes wide with fear. He pushed down harder on the gas pedal.

As I looked out into the purple darkness, a low orange sun began to show over the green treetops. "Where are our parents?" I asked anxiously.

"There's a kind of outdoor theater next to the cemetery," Mr. Dawes said, staring straight ahead through the windshield, his eyes narrow, his expression tense. "It's built right into the ground, and it's hidden by a big tree. I left them there. I told them not to move. I think they'll be safe. I don't think anyone'll think to look there."

"We've seen it," Josh said. A bright light suddenly flashed on in the backseat.

"What's that?" Mr. Dawes asked, looking into the rearview mirror.

"My flashlight," Josh answered, clicking it off. "I brought it just in case. But the sun will be up soon. I probably won't need it."

Mr. Dawes hit the brake and pulled the car to the side of the road. We were at the edge of the cemetery. I climbed quickly out of the car, eager to see my parents.

The sky was still dark, streaked with violet now. The sun was a dark orange balloon just barely poking over the trees. Across the street, beyond the jagged rows of gravestones, I could see the dark outline of the leaning tree that hid the mysterious amphitheater.

"Hurry," Mr. Dawes urged, closing his car door quietly. "I'm sure your parents are desperate to see you."

We headed across the street, half-walking, half-jogging, Josh swinging the flashlight in one hand.

Suddenly, at the edge of the cemetery grass, Josh stopped. "Petey!" he cried.

I followed his gaze and saw our white terrier walking slowly along a slope of gravestones.

"Petey!" Josh yelled again, and began running to the dog.

My heart sank. I hadn't had a chance to tell Josh what Ray had revealed to me about Petey. "No — Josh!" I called.

Mr. Dawes looked very alarmed. "We don't have time. We have to hurry," he said to me. Then he began shouting for Josh to come back.

"I'll go get him," I said, and took off, running as fast as I could along the rows of graves, calling to my brother. "Josh! Josh, wait up! Don't! Don't go after him! Josh — Petey is *dead*!"

Josh had been gaining on the dog, which was ambling along, sniffing the ground, not looking up, not paying any attention to Josh. Then suddenly, Josh tripped over a low grave marker.

He cried out as he fell, and the flashlight flew out of his hand and clattered against a gravestone.

I quickly caught up with him. "Josh — are you okay?"

He was lying on his stomach, staring straight ahead.

"Josh — answer me. Are you okay?"

I grabbed him by the shoulders and tried to pull him up, but he kept staring straight ahead, his mouth open, his eyes wide.

"Josh?"

"Look," he said finally.

I breathed a sigh of relief, knowing that Josh wasn't knocked out or something.

"Look," he repeated, and pointed to the gravestone he had tripped over.

I turned and squinted at the grave. I read the inscription, silently mouthing the words as I read:

COMPTON DAWES, R.I.P. 1966–1996.

My head began to spin. I felt dizzy. I steadied myself, holding onto Josh.

COMPTON DAWES.

It wasn't his father or his grandfather. He had told us he was the only Compton in his family.

So Mr. Dawes was dead, too.

Dead. Dead. Dead.

Dead as everyone else.

He was one of them. One of the dead ones.

Josh and I stared at each other in the purple darkness. Surrounded. Surrounded by the dead.

*Now what?* I asked myself.

*Now what?*

# 16

"Get up, Josh," I said, my voice a choked whisper. "We've got to get away from here."

But we were too late.

A hand grabbed me firmly by the shoulder.

I spun around to see Mr. Dawes, his eyes narrowing as he read the inscription on his own gravestone.

"Mr. Dawes — you, too!" I cried, so disappointed, so confused, so . . . scared.

"Me, too," he said, almost sadly. "All of us." His eyes burned into mine. "This was a normal town once. And we were normal people. Most of us worked in the plastics factory on the outskirts of town. Then there was an accident. Something escaped from the factory. A yellow gas. It floated over the town. So fast we didn't see it . . . didn't realize. And then, it was too late, and Dark Falls wasn't a normal town anymore. We were all dead, Amanda. Dead and buried. But we couldn't rest. We couldn't sleep. Dark Falls was a town of the living dead."

"What — what are you going to do to us?" I managed to ask. My knees were trembling so hard, I could barely stand. A dead man was squeezing my shoulder. A dead man was staring hard into my eyes.

Standing this close, I could smell his sour breath. I turned my head, but the smell already choked my nostrils.

"Where are Mom and Dad?" Josh asked, climbing to his feet and standing rigidly across from us, glaring accusingly at Mr. Dawes.

"Safe and sound," Mr. Dawes said with a faint smile. "Come with me. It's time for you to join them."

I tried to pull away from him, but his hand was locked on my shoulder. "Let go!" I shouted.

His smile grew wider. "Amanda, it doesn't hurt to die," he said softly, almost soothingly. "Come with me."

"No!" Josh shouted. And with sudden quickness, he dived to the ground and picked up his flashlight.

"Yes!" I cried. "Shine it on him, Josh!" The light could save us. The light could defeat Mr. Dawes, as it had Ray. The light could destroy him. "Quick — shine it on him!" I pleaded.

Josh fumbled with the flashlight, then pointed

it toward Mr. Dawes's startled face and clicked
it on.

Nothing.

No light.

"It — it's broken," Josh said. "I guess when it
hit the gravestone . . ."

My heart pounding. I looked back at Mr. Dawes.
The smile on his face was a smile of victory.

"Nice try," Mr. Dawes said to Josh. The smile faded quickly from his face.

Close up, he didn't look so young and handsome. His skin, I could see, was dry and peeling and hung loosely beneath his eyes.

"Let's go, kids," he said, giving me a shove. He glanced up at the brightening sky. The sun was raising itself over the treetops.

Josh hesitated.

"I *said* let's go," Mr. Dawes snapped impatiently. He loosened his grip on my shoulder and took a menacing step toward Josh.

Josh glanced down at the worthless flashlight. Then he pulled his arm back and heaved the flashlight at Mr. Dawes's head.

The flashlight hit its target with a sickening *crack*. It hit Mr. Dawes in the center of his forehead, splitting a large hole in the skin.

Mr. Dawes uttered a low cry. His eyes widened in surprise. Dazed, he reached a hand up to the hole where a few inches of gray skull poked through.

"Run, Josh!" I cried.

But there was no need to tell him that. He was already zigzagging through the rows of graves, his head ducked low. I followed him, running as fast as I could.

Glancing back, I saw Mr. Dawes stagger after us, still holding his ripped forehead. He took several steps, then abruptly stopped, staring up at the sky.

*It's too bright for him,* I realized. *He has to stay in the shade.*

Josh had ducked down behind a tall marble monument, old and slightly tilted, cracked down the middle. I slid down beside him, gasping for breath.

Leaning on the cool marble, we both peered around the sides of the monument. Mr. Dawes, a scowl on his face, was heading back toward the amphitheater, keeping in the shadows of the trees.

"He's — he's not chasing us," Josh whispered, his chest heaving as he struggled to catch his breath and stifle his fear. "He's going back."

"The sun is too bright for him," I said, holding on to the side of the monument. "He must be going to get Mom and Dad."

"That stupid flashlight," Josh cried.

"Never mind that," I said, watching Mr. Dawes until he disappeared behind the big leaning tree. "What are we going to do now? I don't know —"

"*Shhh.* Look!" Josh poked me hard on the shoulder and pointed. "Who's that?"

I followed his stare and saw several dark figures hurrying through the rows of tombstones. They seemed to have appeared from out of nowhere.

Did they rise out of the graves?

Walking quickly, seeming to float over the green, sloping ground, they headed into the shadows. All were walking in silence, their eyes straight ahead. They didn't stop to greet one another. They strode purposefully toward the hidden amphitheater, as if they were being drawn there, as if they were puppets being pulled by hidden strings.

"Whoa. Look at them all!" Josh whispered, ducking his head back behind the marble monument.

The dark moving forms made all the shadows ripple. It looked as if the trees, the gravestones, the entire cemetery had come to life, had started toward the hidden seats of the amphitheater.

"There goes Karen," I whispered, pointing. "And George. And all the rest of them."

The kids from our house were moving quickly in twos and threes, following the other shadows, as silent and businesslike as everyone else.

*Everyone was here except Ray*, I thought.

*Because we killed Ray.*

*We killed someone who was already dead.*

"Do you think Mom and Dad are really down in that weird theater?" Josh asked, interrupting my morbid thoughts, his eyes on the moving shadows.

"Come on," I said, taking Josh's hand and pulling him away from the monument. "We've got to find out."

We watched the last of the dark figures float past the enormous leaning tree. The shadows stopped moving. The cemetery was still and silent. A solitary crow floated high above in the clear blue, cloudless sky.

Slowly, Josh and I edged our way toward the amphitheater, ducking behind gravestones, keeping low to the ground.

It was a struggle to move. I felt as if I weighed five hundred pounds. The weight of my fear, I guess.

I was desperate to see if Mom and Dad were there.

But at the same time, I didn't want to see.

I didn't want to see them held prisoner by Mr. Dawes and the others.

I didn't want to see them . . . killed.

The thought made me stop. I reached out an arm and halted Josh.

We were standing behind the leaning tree, hidden by its enormous clump of upraised roots. Beyond the tree, down in the theater below, I could hear the low murmur of voices.

"Are Mom and Dad there?" Josh whispered. He started to poke his head around the side of the bent tree trunk, but I cautiously pulled him back.

"Be careful," I whispered. "Don't let them see you. They're practically right beneath us."

"But I've *got* to know if Mom and Dad are really here," he whispered, his eyes frightened, pleading.

"Me, too," I agreed.

We both leaned over the massive trunk. The bark felt smooth under my hands as I gazed into the deep shadows cast by the tree.

And then I saw them.

Mom and Dad. They were tied up, back-to-back, standing in the center of the floor at the bottom of the amphitheater in front of everyone.

They looked so uncomfortable, so terrified. Their arms were tied down tightly at their sides. Dad's face was bright red. Mom's hair was all messed up, hanging wildly down over her forehead, her head bowed.

Squinting into the darkness cast by the tree, I saw Mr. Dawes standing beside them along with another, older man. And I saw that the rows of long benches built into the ground were filled with people. Not a single empty space.

*Everyone in town must be here*, I realized.

*Everyone except Josh and me.*

"They're going to kill Mom and Dad," Josh whispered, grabbing my arm, squeezing it in fear. "They're going to make Mom and Dad just like them."

"Then they'll come after us," I said, thinking out loud, staring through the shadows at my poor parents. Both of them had their heads bowed now as they stood before the silent crowd. Both of them were awaiting their fate.

"What are we going to do?" Josh whispered.

"Huh?" I was staring so hard at Mom and Dad, I guess I momentarily blanked out.

"What are we going to do?" Josh repeated urgently, still holding desperately to my arm. "We can't just stand here and —"

I suddenly knew what we were going to do.

It just came to me. I didn't even have to think hard.

"Maybe we can save them," I whispered, backing away from the tree. "Maybe we *can* do something."

Josh let go of my arm. He stared at me eagerly.

"We're going to push this tree over," I whispered with so much confidence that I surprised myself. "We're going to push the tree over so the sunlight will fill the amphitheater."

"Yes!" Josh cried immediately. "Look at this tree. It's practically down already. We can do it!"

I *knew* we could do it. I don't know where my confidence came from. But I *knew* we could do it.

And I knew we had to do it fast.

Peering over the top of the trunk again, struggling to see through the shadows, I could see that everyone in the theater had stood up. They were all starting to move forward, down toward Mom and Dad.

"Come on, Josh," I whispered. "We'll take a running jump and push the tree over. Come on!"

Without another word, we both took several steps back.

We just had to give the trunk a good, hard push, and the tree would topple right over. The roots were already almost entirely up out of the ground, after all.

One hard push. That's all it would take. And the sunlight would pour into the theater. Beautiful, golden sunlight. Bright, bright sunlight.

The dead people would all crumble.

And Mom and Dad would be saved.

All four of us would be saved.

"Come on, Josh," I whispered. "Ready?"

He nodded, his face solemn, his eyes frightened.

"Okay. Let's *go!*" I cried.

We both ran forward, digging our sneakers into the ground, moving as fast as we could, our arms outstretched and ready.

In a second, we hit the tree trunk and pushed with all of our strength, shoving it with our hands and then moving our shoulders into it, pushing . . . pushing . . . pushing . . .

It didn't budge.

"Push!" I cried. "Push it again!"

Josh let out an exasperated, defeated sigh. "I can't, Amanda. I can't move it."

"Josh —" I glared at him.

He backed up to try again.

Below, I could hear startled voices, angry voices.

"Quick!" I yelled. *"Push!"*

We hurtled into the tree trunk with our shoulders, both of us grunting from the effort, our muscles straining, our faces bright red.

"Push! Keep pushing!"

The veins at my temples felt about to pop.

Was the tree moving?

No.

It gave a little but bounced right back.

The voices from below were getting louder.

"We can't do it!" I cried, so disappointed, so frustrated, so terrified. "We can't move it!"

Defeated, I slumped over onto the tree trunk and started to bury my face in my hands.

I pulled back with a gasp when I heard the soft cracking sound. The cracking grew louder until it was a rumble, then a roar. It sounded as if the ground were ripping apart.

The old tree fell quickly. It didn't have far to fall. But it hit with a thundering crash that seemed to shake the ground.

I grabbed Josh and we both stood in amazement and disbelief as bright sunlight poured into the amphitheater.

The cries went up instantly. Horrified cries. Angry cries. Frantic cries.

The cries became howls. Howls of pain, of agony.

The people in the amphitheater, the living dead caught in the golden light, began scrambling over one another, screeching, pulling, climbing, pushing, trying to claw their way to shade.

But it was too late.

Their skin began to drop off their bones and, as I stared openmouthed, they crumbled to powder and dissolved to the ground, their clothes disintegrating along with them.

The painful cries continued to ring out as the bodies fell apart, the skin melted away, the dry bones collapsed. I saw Karen Somerset staggering across the floor. I saw her hair fall to the ground in a heap, revealing the dark skull underneath. She cast a glance up at me, a longing look, a look of regret. And then her eyeballs rolled out of their sockets, and she opened her toothless mouth and cried, "Thank you, Amanda! Thank you!" and collapsed.

Josh and I covered our ears to shut out the ghastly cries. We both looked away, unable to keep watching the entire town fall in agony and crumble to powder, destroyed by the sun, the clear, warm sun.

When we looked back, they had all disappeared.

Mom and Dad were standing right where they had been, tied back-to-back, their expressions a mixture of horror and disbelief.

"Mom! Dad!" I cried.

I'll never forget their smiles as Josh and I ran forward to free them.

It didn't take our parents long to get us packed up and to arrange for the movers to take us back to our old neighborhood and our old house. "I guess it's lucky after all that we couldn't sell the old place," Dad said as we eagerly piled into the car to leave.

Dad backed down the driveway and started to roar away.

"Stop!" I cried suddenly. I'm not sure why, but I had a sudden, powerful urge to take one last look at the old house.

As both of my parents called out to me in confusion, I pushed open the door and jogged back to the driveway. Standing in the middle of the yard, I stared up at the house, silent, empty, still covered in thick layers of blue-gray shadows.

I found myself gazing up at the old house as if I were hypnotized. I don't know how long I stood there.

The crunch of tires on the gravel driveway snapped me out of my spell. Startled, I turned to see a red station wagon parked in the driveway.

Two boys about Josh's age jumped out of the back. Their parents followed. Staring up at the house, they didn't seem to notice me.

"Here we are, kids," the mother said, smiling at them. "Our new house."

"It doesn't look new. It looks old," one of the boys said.

And then his brother's eyes widened as he noticed me. "Who are *you*?" he demanded.

The other members of his family turned to stare at me.

"Oh. I . . . uh . . ." His question caught me by surprise. I could hear my dad honking his horn impatiently down on the street. "I . . . uh . . . used to live in your house," I found myself answering.

And then I turned and ran full speed down to the street.

*Wasn't that Mr. Dawes standing at the porch,*

*clipboard in hand?* I wondered, catching a glimpse of a dark figure as I ran to the car.

*No, it couldn't be Mr. Dawes up there waiting for them,* I decided.

*It just couldn't be.*

I didn't look back. I slammed the car door behind me, and we sped away.

# BEHIND THE SCREAMS

# WELCOME TO DEAD HOUSE

## CONTENTS

Bonus material written and compiled
by Matthew D. Payne

## About the Author

R.L. Stine's books are read all over the world. So far, his books have sold more than 300 million copies, making him one of the most popular children's authors in history. Besides Goosebumps, R.L. Stine has written the teen series Fear Street, the funny series Rotten School, as well as the Mostly Ghostly series, The Nightmare Room series, and the two-book thriller *Dangerous Girls*. R.L. Stine lives in New York with his wife, Jane, and Minnie, his King Charles spaniel. You can learn more about him at www.RLStine.com.

# Q & A with R.L. Stine

Petey, the family's white terrier, knew something was fishy in Dark Falls before the human members of the family did. As Ray, one of the creepy neighborhood kids, said in Chapter 13, "Dogs always know." Has your pooch, or any of your friends' pooches, ever detected ghosts or ghouls?

R.L. Stine (RLS): *I can't say that my dog has ever detected a ghost — but I do think that dogs have a kind of sensitivity to the world that can be a little creepy. My dog is so terrified of thunder and lightning that she always hides in the closet when there is a storm. But recently we noticed that almost an hour before the storm starts — even if the sun is shining — poor Minnie heads for the closet. Dogs know things. . . .*

Eleven-year-old Josh was fearless the night he went to the cemetery to find Petey. When you were Josh's age, could you have walked through a cemetery in the dead of night without getting scared?

RLS: *No! But when I was a kid, there was a big pile of white stones behind my house. My brother and I believed that there were dead people buried under those stones. One Halloween my brother and I decided to go to the mound of stones and wait for ghosts. I remember the moon was full, and the stones sparkled* in the moonlight. *My brother and I inched our way close to the mound and then we looked at each other and ran home! It was too scary.*

You're an incredibly well-known — and well-read! — children's book author. The Goosebumps series has sold over 300 million copies! You must have tons of people come to hear you read. What's the biggest crowd or longest line you've ever had at a book signing?

RLS: *Once I was doing a signing in Columbus, Ohio, where I grew up. I was driving to the bookstore and I got stuck in a huge traffic jam. I was really upset because I knew that if the traffic didn't ease up, I'd be late for the signing. Finally, I yelled out the window to a policeman to find out what was causing the traffic jam. The answer amazed me. I was the cause of the traffic jam! So many people showed up to see me that the street was totally blocked. That was cool!*

If you weren't an author, what career path do you think you would have followed?

RLS: *I always wanted to be a cartoonist. But there's a problem with that. I can't draw.*

It's one thing to write, but another thing to come up with ideas to write about. Without ideas, you can't write about anything!

How do you keep coming up with new ideas and creepy creatures year after year?

RLS: *I really don't know. Ideas come from every-where. But most of the time, I think of a title for a book — then the idea starts to take shape in my mind. For instance, Goosebumps HorrorLand #13:* When the Ghost Dog Howls. *Having that title makes me think: When does the dog howl? And why is he a ghost? And where does he come from? Answering those questions gives me the start of a story. I hope you like the book. Here's a secret: I'm writing a bunch more HorrorLand books with new villains, new attractions, and new scares.*

Speaking of the next HorrorLand book, most people think of hamsters as cute, cuddly pets, but your stories tend to go in a different direction. What do you have in store for readers with HorrorLand # 14: *Little Shop of Hamsters?*

RLS: *Sure, everyone thinks hamsters are cute and cuddly — but that's just an act! The hamsters in* Little Shop of Hamsters *look cute, but here's some advice: Don't get them mad!*

To find out if R.L. Stine could survive in the wild, grab a copy of the new collector's edition of **GOOSEBUMPS: WELCOME TO CAMP NIGHTMARE**, and LOOK in the back of the BOOK.

# Hungry . . . for YOU!

Bloodsuckers! Brain eaters! The children in *Welcome to Dead House* are just a few of the many creatures, dead and living, who can all agree that YOU are their favorite food. Hopefully, you won't run into the hideous creatures on this list.

| HIDEOUS CREATURE | DEAD OR LIVING? | FAVORITE FOOD | IF BITTEN . . . |
|---|---|---|---|
| Mosquito | Living | Your blood! | Get ready to scratch! In some places, a mosquito's bite can also transmit diseases. |
| Vampire | Undead | Your blood! | You will turn into a vampire! |
| Werewolf | Living | Your flesh! | You will turn into a werewolf. Unless the werewolf eats ALL of you! |
| Zombie | Dead | Your brains! | You will turn into a zombie. Unless a pack of zombies tears you limb from limb. |
| Tick | Living | Your blood! | You have to remove the tick without pulling OFF its head, which can stay under your skin. |
| *N. fowleri* Amoeba | Living | Your brains! | We're not sure if amoebas bite, but if this critter gets into your brain, there is very, very little chance for survival. |

# Cemeteries: Come for a Visit . . . Stay for ETERNITY

The cemetery in Dark Falls is super-creepy at night. Most cemeteries are scary . . . even without the **LIVING DEAD** roaming around! During the day, though, cemeteries are actually a great place to head for some peace. In most cities and towns, it's the only area where things are completely **QUIET!** Everyone just lies around and relaxes . . . **SIX FEET** under the ground.

The cemeteries we see today are larger versions of the **GRAVEYARDS** that are found in old churchyards. The dead were buried in church grounds with markers or headstones at the grave sites. The only problem was, these small churches ran out of space — **CORPSES** were piled up on one another in the graves!

In addition to the space crunch, having the dead so close to the living, especially in large cities, helped to spread **DISEASE**. Cities realized this and placed a ban on burials. Soon, massive cemeteries were built outside of cities.

One such cemetery is Green-Wood in Brooklyn, New York. It is so large and beautiful that since its creation in 1838, people have been going there to relax, sightsee, and just walk around. When New York City's **CENTRAL PARK** opened decades later, many said it looked just like Green-Wood . . . without the **TOMBSTONES!**

Still, there's just something SOOO creepy about being surrounded by so many **DEAD PEOPLE**. As the saying goes, "It's quiet . . . **TOO** quiet!" Generally, cemeteries are not a place to be at night: The risk of hitting your knee on a tombstone (and that really bruises) or falling into an **OPEN GRAVE** are reasons enough to stay away. Plus, there have been numerous reports of **CEMETERY HAUNTINGS** across the U.S. Moaning or weeping can be heard from inside large **CRYPTS**. Onlookers have seen strange mists on clear nights. People born hundreds of years ago have been seen going for a late-night walk together.

Perhaps the most terrifying tomb tale is about The Voodoo Queen of New Orleans, buried in the St. Louis Cemetery #1. Since her death in 1881, there have been numerous sightings of her ghost. Legend has it that you can hear her casting a **CURSE** on those who trespass within the cemetery walls and vandalize gravestones. Many people have reported seeing her in the form of a **BLACK CAT** walking amongst the graves. Don't let her see your back or you'll be cursed to do her bidding for eternity!

The scariest thing of all: Soon there won't be any more room left in places like Green-Wood to comfortably bury anyone! Some interesting solutions to this problem have been found. For instance, several **SKYSCRAPER CEMETERIES** have been built in South America. Dozens of floors high, they offer the tradition of tomb burial while saving a whole lot of space. So will there soon be an R.L. Stine book on the horrors of being locked in a skyscraper cemetery at night? We shall see. . . .

The largest cemetery in the world (according to the *Guinness Book of World Records*) is the Ohlsdorf Cemetery in Hamburg, Germany. Covering an area of almost 1,000 acres, it has nearly 1.4 million "residents."

Not every culture buries its dead. One of the creepier traditions was found in ancient Persia. Followers of Zoroastrianism used to gather the dead in huge "Towers of Silence," where **FLESH-EATING BIRDS** like vultures picked away at the corpses until only the **BONES** were left.

# Which House Is Haunted?

Read the descriptions of five different haunted houses. Some are real haunted houses, but two are houses that R.L. Stine created for his terrifying tales. Can you tell which haunted houses are real and which are made up by R.L. Stine? Write your answers on a piece of paper and use the key at the bottom of the facing page to see if you're right. If you can't pick out the two R.L. Stine houses, you need to read more Goosebumps!

**1** A family moves out of their house after a poltergeist breaks photo frames, messes up the furniture, and even melts a phone! Eventually, the family comes back home and defeats the ghost.

**2** One night, the Payne family abandons their home, and the neighbors never hear from them again. Kids passing by the house on Halloween night dare each other to break in and have a terrifying run-in with a demon dog!

**3** The Lutz family moves into a house whose previous inhabitants were murdered. Soon after, crazy things start to happen — green ooze pours out of the walls, flies are everywhere (even in the winter), and faces appear in the fireplace.

**4** After their baby dies, a young couple lock themselves in their house and spend the rest of their lives bitter and arguing. After they die, they haunt the house and turn any children who come inside into ghosts!

**5** A famous gun maker's wife is haunted by the ghosts of the people killed by his guns. She is forced to move and build a new, bigger house — and must continue to build more and more rooms for them to haunt, or she'll die!

# CREATE YOUR OWN HAUNTED HOUSE TALE!

**Start the story below by choosing words, adding a friend's name, and filling in the missing sentence. Then use the rest of the space to keep the story going! Remember — be scary AND funny!**

I don't want to believe it, but I think my house is haunted! I'm not surprised, since we live next to [a cemetery] [a mad scientist who is experimenting on humans] [a ghost factory]. As soon as we moved in a year ago, I knew something [creepy] [disgusting] [annoying] would come from over there and [haunt] [entertain] [bother] us.

There are a few reasons I can tell my house is [under the spell of a poltergeist] [haunted] [turning into a loony bin for ghosts]. For one thing, my [kitchen] [living room] [basement] is totally [spooky] [scary] [smelly], especially [when it's raining] [at night] [when I'm trying to practice my dance moves]! Just the other day, I was [eating] [shaving the dog] [doing my homework] in there when suddenly I heard [moaning] [whispers] [the ghost of Elvis]. Nobody else was around, so I was really scared. It sounded so real! So I pulled out my cell phone and called my best friend, _____.

I said, "_____!"

My best friend, _____ , got so freaked out that [he] [she] decided to come over and help me investigate. As soon as [he] [she] got there, we [ate some Brussels sprouts] [put on biohazard suits] [listened really hard for the sound again]. We must have been in there for an hour, but nothing happened. Then we heard something coming from [the bathroom] [the garage] [my room]. It sounded like [whispering] [a sad and angry moan] [creepy old music].

We rushed toward the sound and found . . .

_____

_____

_____

_____

_____

_____

_____

_____

_____

_____

_____

_____

_____

_____

_____

_____

_____

_____

_____

_____

_____

_____

_____

_____

**Still going . . . ? Go to your computer or grab more paper to make your story as long as you want. Maybe it will become a book one day!**

# Add more Goosebumps to your collection!
## Here's a chilling preview of

## LITTLE SHOP OF HAMSTERS

# The adventure continues in the world's scariest theme park!

# 6

I pressed the POWER button and popped a round orange candy into my mouth. "Want one? They're really sour." I raised the phone to Lexi.

She made a disgusted face and shoved my hand away. "You know sour candy makes me puke. One candy and I'll puke all over your shoes."

"Thanks for sharing that," I said. I popped another one into my mouth. Then I tucked the phone into the pocket of my T-shirt.

It was a warm, sunny Saturday afternoon. We'd been back home for a week. I met Lexi after her tennis lesson at City Courts, and we were walking toward my house.

She wore white tennis shorts and a silky gray vest over a white T-shirt. Her hair was still damp from her tennis game.

A blue-and-red neon sign over a little store caught my attention. It was glowing brightly even in the strong sunshine. LITTLE SHOP OF HAMSTERS.

"Is that a new pet store?" I asked.

I didn't wait for her answer. I tore across the street. Two teenagers on bikes swerved to miss me. They screamed some rude words and shook their fists at me.

I love pet stores. I eagerly peered through the glass door, but I couldn't see anything inside. I pushed the door open and stepped into the shop. Lexi hurried in right behind me.

The store was dark inside. The air felt hot and steamy. It smelled like a barn. Like straw and dirt and farm animals. A slowly spinning ceiling fan made the deep shadows dance in front of us.

"Whoa!" I let out a startled cry as I nearly bumped into a glass wall. I blinked and let my eyes adjust to the dim light.

An enormous display case filled the center of the shop. It had glass walls on all four sides and a glass top. A narrow sliding wire door was placed in one of the glass walls.

The case was taller than me. It had to be at least six feet tall. And it was nearly as wide as the store.

From inside the walls of glass, eyes stared out at me. Dozens of tiny black eyes. The case was actually a cage! It had *hundreds* of hamsters packed inside.

Hamsters poked their noses against the glass, gazing out at Lexi and me. Behind them, hamsters scampered through the wood shavings that covered the cage floor.

What was that strange squeaking sound? Hamster wheels. I counted eight or ten of them, with hamsters running hard, making them spin and squeal.

Hamsters were chomping away in the long row of food dishes on the sides. Others ran through long, twisting plastic tubes. One big guy was trying to climb a side of the glass cage. Two hamsters were wrestling in a food dish.

"Lexi — it's like a big hamster circus!" I said.

She pressed her hands against the glass and peered in. "You mean like a hamster *city*!" she said. "The cage is bigger than my bedroom!"

"They are totally cute," I said. "Look how they wrinkle their noses."

She poked me. "Hey — check out the funny front teeth. That one looks just like you, Sam!"

"Ha-ha," I said, poking her back. "What a weird store. No dogs or birds or anything. Just hamsters. Hundreds of hamsters."

"Look. That one found a piece of carrot," Lexi said, pointing. "And the big brown one is waiting for him to drop it. Ready to pounce. This is a total riot!"

I watched a cute little gray hamster running on a wheel. The squeaking wheels were the only sounds in the shop, except for the hum of the ceiling fan.

"My parents won't let me get a dog," I told Lexi. "They say I have to prove I'm responsible first."

"Like I don't know that," Lexi said, staring into the cage. "Sam, you've told me that a thousand times!"

"But maybe they'll let me get a hamster," I said. "You don't have to walk a hamster or anything. It doesn't take much work."

Lexi started to answer. But her mouth dropped open and no sound came out. Her eyes bulged.

I turned and followed her gaze. And then I gasped as I squinted into the dim light and saw what she was staring at.

An *enormous* hamster — gigantic! — taller than Lexi and me — crept out from behind the cage. It walked on *two legs*, in a strange, shuffling motion.

Its glassy eyes — as big as tennis balls! — gazed straight ahead. Its huge front paws swung low at its bulging sides. Its fur ruffled by the wind from the ceiling fan.

It turned. It SAW us!

And its big paws thudded softly on the floor as it headed right for us!

"No!" A sharp cry escaped my throat.

The creature's huge eyes didn't blink. They stared hard at Lexi and me, glowing darkly.

The giant hamster moved in and out of the shadows cast down from the spinning ceiling fan. Lexi and I backed up against the glass cage. And watched it slowly advance, step by step.

And then it reached up with its big white front paws and lifted off its head.

Lexi and I burst out laughing.

A man in a hamster costume! He held the head in front of him. His face was red, and his forehead was dripping with sweat.

"Hot in this thing," he said.

His curly black-and-gray hair was drenched. He had dark eyes, a big round nose, and a bushy black mustache that looked like a paintbrush.

He set the hamster head down on the front counter. "Like my new store?" he asked. He pulled his arms free and climbed out of the costume.

"I'm Mr. Fitz." He was short and thin, but he had a deep voice. He put a white apron on and struggled to tie the straps. "Your names?"

We told him.

"Do you wear that costume all day long?" Lexi asked.

He picked up a towel and mopped his face and hair. "No," he said. "Just sometimes. It's an attention getter."

"Sure is," I said. "You really got *our* attention!" I decided not to tell him he nearly scared us to death!

"I wear it outside the shop to attract customers," Fitz said. "When you have a new store, you have to work hard to get people to notice you."

He shoved the costume under the counter.

"I like your store," I said. "It's totally cool."

"Sam is really into animals," Lexi said.

Fitz nodded. "Is that so?" He opened the wire door to the glass cage. A few hamsters turned at the sound. The rest went on with what they were doing.

Fitz reached into the wood shavings and pulled up a hamster in each hand. Then he turned and handed one to Lexi and one to me.

My hamster was white with brown spots down his back. He squirmed in my hand. I almost dropped him. His pink nose twitched, and he gazed up at me with bright black eyes.

Lexi rubbed a finger down the back of her

hamster. He was all white, except for a scattering of little brown spots on his face. They kind of looked like freckles.

"I love their fur," she said. "So soft." The hamster tried to nibble her finger. She turned it around in her hand.

"Totally awesome," I told Fitz.

He motioned to the little guy, who was trying to climb up my arm. "Do you want him, Sam? They're not very expensive."

"I wish," I said with a sigh. "I'd love a hamster. But my parents won't let me have a pet."

"He has to prove he's responsible first," Lexi chimed in.

Fitz eyed me. "You're not very responsible?"

"Yes, I am," I said. "It's just . . . they want me to prove I'd take good care of a pet."

Fitz nodded. "Well, you can come back here anytime and play with them."

The hamster tickled my hand with his nose. I handed him back to Fitz. "Thanks."

Lexi petted her hamster a little more, then she carried him to the cage  and set him down. We started to the front door.

But Fitz stopped us. "Hey — want to help me give them water? I've got a lot of water bottles to fill."

He pulled two glass bottles from behind the counter.

"Sure," I said. I took one of them from him. "What's in this bottle? Just plain water?"

"It's called Vito-Vigor," Fitz answered. "It's vitamin water. You know. Like you buy at the supermarket."

He handed Lexi the other bottle of Vito-Vigor. Then he led us to the back of the cage. "Pour the water into these tubes," he said. "It runs into their water bottles."

I tilted the bottle and poured water into the tube that stuck out of the back of the cage. I could see it flow into the bottle on the other side of the glass.

"You have to go inside the cage to feed them and change the floor shavings," Fitz said.

"Look at them all staring up at us. They must think we're *giants* or something," Lexi said.

"Maybe they think we're *monsters*," I said. "Maybe they'll have nightmares about us."

Lexi laughed. "Sam, I *already* have nightmares about you!"

We filled all the water bottles, then handed Fitz the empty Vito-Vigor bottles.

"Well, thanks for your help, guys" he said. "Come back anytime."

The bell on top of the front door jingled as we walked out. We turned and started toward my house.

Lexi had a strange smile on her face. She had

her arms wrapped tightly around the front of her vest.

We walked a few blocks, then she stopped. Her eyes flashed and her grin grew wider.

"Here, Sam," she said, "here's a present for you." She held out her hand.

And I let out a scream. "Lexi — are you CRAZY?"

# DOUBLE THE FRIGHT ALL AT ONE SITE

## www.scholastic.com/goosebumps

FIENDS OF GOOSEBUMPS &
GOOSEBUMPS HORRORLAND CAN:

- PLAY GHOULISH GAMES!

- CHAT WITH FELLOW FAN-ATICS!

- WATCH CLIPS FROM SPINE-TINGLING DVDs!

- EXPLORE CLASSIC BOOKS AND NEW TERROR-IFIC TITLES!

- CHECK OUT THE GOOSEBUMPS HORRORLAND VIDEO GAME!

- GET GOOSEBUMPS PHOTOSHOCK FOR THE IPHONE™
  OR IPOD TOUCH®!

▲ SCHOLASTIC

GBWEB

# The Original Bone-Chilling
# Goosebumps®
## Series